The Elson Readers—Book Three
A Teacher's Guide

◆

Michele Black
B.A., Elementary Education; Elementary Teacher/Babson Park Elementary School

Cynthia Keel Landen
M.A., Educational Leadership; B.A., Early Childhood and Elementary Education; Elementary Teacher/Babson Park Elementary School

Lorrie Driggers Phillips
M.A., Curriculum and Instruction; B.A., Early Childhood and Elementary Education; Elementary Teacher/Babson Park Elementary School

Lost Classics
Book Company
Lake Wales, Florida

PUBLISHER'S NOTE

Recognizing the need to return to more traditional principles in education, Lost Classics Book Company is republishing forgotten late 19th and early 20th century literature and textbooks to aid parents in the education of their children.

The Elson Readers—Book Three, which this volume is meant to accompany, has been assigned a reading level of 750L. More information concerning this reading level assessment may be attained by visiting www.lexile.com.

The Authors

Michele Denise Black graduated from Warner Southern College with a degree in elementary education. She has been teaching for eleven years with the Polk County School System in Florida. She is also an instructor at Warner Southern College during their summer English program where she teaches conversational English to Japanese high school students. She is currently teaching fifth grade at Babson Park Elementary School in Babson Park, Florida.

Cynthia Keel Landen graduated with degrees in early childhood and elementary education from the University of Florida. She earned her master's degree in educational leadership at the University of South Florida. She is an elementary teacher with eighteen years of experience and is currently teaching fifth grade at Babson Park Elementary School in Babson Park, Florida.

Lorrie Driggers Phillips graduated from Florida Southern College with degrees in early childhood and elementary education. She received her master's degree in curriculum and instruction from the University of Southern Mississippi. She taught for thirteen years.

© Copyright 2005
Lost Classics Book Company
ISBN 978-1-890623-27-2
Designed to Accompany
The Elson Readers—Book Two
ISBN 978-1-890623-17-2
Part of *The Elson Readers*
Nine Volumes: *Primer* through *Book Eight*
ISBN 978-1-890623-23-4

On the Cover:
Joseph, Overseer of the Pharoahs
by Sir Lawrence Tadema (1836-1912)
Private Collection/Bridgeman Art Library

TABLE OF CONTENTS

THE ELSON READERS—BOOK THREE
A TEACHER'S GUIDE

FOREWORD

Lists of words will be provided for each story. We suggest that your child learn these words prior to reading the stories. One way of teaching the words is for your child to write one word at the top of a page in a vocabulary journal. Your child can then draw a picture that illustrates the word and use the word in a sentence on the same page. Another method for learning and reviewing the vocabulary words is by using index cards. The words can go on one side of the card and the pictures and sentences on the other. These cards are great for reviewing all the words.

You will find comprehension questions for most of the stories. Unlike the previous texts, these questions will not be labeled. This is a transitional stage in a few ways. Students at this level have had many experiences in answering comprehension questions and are familiar with types of questions without the labels. Students should be expected to answer these questions on paper in complete sentences.

Another way that this is a transition is that there are fewer phonic lessons. Children at this level have generally mastered the sounds of the English language. There will be a review of the long and short vowel sounds. There will be lessons on grammar and word usage.

Continue to research topics of interest by using the library or the computer. Turn the newly found information into a writing project. This guide has many lessons in all types of writing.

Research shows that reading to your child is the best way to promote successful reading. For the greatest results, read to your child daily. Let your child pick the books or stories you read together. Take turns reading the selected books. Your child can understand something that is two years above his or her own reading level.

THE ELSON READERS—BOOK THREE
A TEACHER'S GUIDE

HOW TO USE THIS BOOK

The *Elson Readers, Book Three* is filled with enjoyable selections from which your child can learn. The book is organized in the following themes: Fables and Folk Tales, Brownies and Fairies, Children, Legends, Holidays, Home and Country, Heroes of Long Ago, The Outdoor World, and Old Tales. You could start collecting pictures, books, magazines, posters, cards, stuffed animals, puzzles, puppets, and other educational items to go with these themes. These items can be used as learning tools to enhance the stories in this book.

Lists of words will be provided for each story. Some of the vocabulary words are words that are related to the story and probably will not be found in a dictionary. Use clues from the selection to determine the intended meaning of these words. We suggest that your child learn these words prior to reading the stories.

You will find comprehension questions for most of the stories. Use the answers provided as a guide on how to answer the comprehension questions.

Language skills are provided for each selection. Answers will also be provided.

At the end of each section in this book there will be a few questions to answer about the stories from that section. You will find them after the comprehension questions for a story, usually the last in the section. Answers will vary for these questions, as most are opinions.

A NOTE ABOUT THIS GUIDE

Teachers and students alike may notice a difference in punctuation, capitalization, and spelling between the prose and poetry sections in the reader. Rules for these matters have changed since the original reader's publication, and we have decided that in the prose sections it would be in the best interest of the student to update these items so they will learn these rules as practiced today. However, the stories remain completely unabridged. We have exercised constraint, and typical changes consist of, for example: commas used in place of semicolons when appropriate, lowercase treatment of words not personified, or hyphenated spelling of words being contracted to modern spellings. We have, however, followed the traditional editorial practice of not changing these items in works of poetry, leaving these matters to the prerogative of the poet.

We have used *The Chicago Manual of Style,* 14th Edition, published by the University of Chicago, as our primary reference for these changes.

Objectives—

By completing *Book Three,* the following objectives will be met:

1. The student will predict what a story is about based on its title and illustrations.
2. The student will identify words and construct meaning from text, illustrations, use of phonics, and context clues.
3. The student will use knowledge of developmental-level vocabulary in reading.
4. The student will increase comprehension by retelling and discussion.
5. The student will determine the main idea and supporting details from text.
6. The student will use simple reference materials to obtain information.
7. The student will show an awareness of a beginning, middle, and end in passages.
8. The student will follow simple sets of instructions for simple tasks using logical sequencing of steps.
9. The student will listen for a variety of purposes, including curiosity, pleasure, getting directions, performing tasks, solving problems, and following rules.
10. The student will retell details of information heard, including sequence of events.
11. The student will determine the main idea through illustrations.
12. The student will recognize basic patterns in and functions of language.
13. The student will understand that word choice can shape ideas, feelings, and actions.
14. The student will identify and use repetition, rhyme, and rhythm in oral and written text.
15. The student will identify the story elements of setting, plot, character, problem, and solution.
16. The student will use text and previous reading to generate predictions.
17. The student will use different forms of words, including prefixes and suffixes.
18. The student will determine author's purpose and character's motives.
19. The student will determine fact from opinion.
20. The student will understand distinguishing features between fiction, drama, poetry, fables, fantasy, biography, and fairy tales.
21. The student will determine how to draw conclusions from text.
22. The student will understand sentence varieties, paragraph writing, and punctuation.
23. The student will use a simple outline.

THE HARE AND THE HEDGEHOG,
p. 7

Preteach the following vocabulary: hedgehog, turnips, rude, hare, cabbage, stupid, proud, ill-tempered, pleasantest, manner, speech, quite, joke, furrows, boast, beaten, willing, surprised, simple, fresh, neighbor, sadly, and juicy.

Answer the following comprehension questions on paper.

1. Why did the hedgehog think the hares were rude? The hedgehog thought the hares were rude because they made fun of the hedgehog's short legs.

2. What did the hare say that made the little hedgehog angry? The hare asked what fun it could be to walk with such short legs.

3. Read the reply of the hedgehog.

4. The hedgehog thought the hare was too proud of his long legs; what did he say he would teach the hare? The hedgehog said he would teach the hare that it does not pay to boast.

5. What word do we sometimes use instead of *boast*? We sometimes use the word *brag* instead of *boast*.

6. Tell the story of the joke that the hedgehogs played on the hare.

7. What did the little hedgehog mean when he said, "Brains are better than legs"? Little hedgehog meant that it was better to be intelligent than to just be a fast runner.

8. This story is a "folk tale"; can you see why folks in different countries told it over and over? People in different countries probably told it over and over because the story is funny while teaching a lesson.

Use the worksheet to practice captions. For a review with the long *a* sound, see if your child can find 15 words in the story with the long *a* sound.

Answers to long *a* words: hare, take, a, said, day, angry, race, may, pay, way, say, play, waiting, place, lay, strange, ate, brains

Answers: Accept reasonable captions. (The answers at the end of each lesson are to the worksheet exercises following each lesson.)

THE HARE AND THE HEDGEHOG, p. 7

Captions are phrases or sentences that describe a picture, graph, or
chart. Before beginning this activity, look at various reading
materials. Pay close attention to the captions used with each
picture or chart. Now, look at the pictures in this story. See if
you can add some captions that are interesting and descriptive.

1. _____

_____

_____

2. _____

_____

_____

3. _____

_____

_____

OLD HORSES KNOW BEST, P. 15

Preteach the following vocabulary: horse, young, drawing, cart, piled, jars, ruts, tumbling, and ditch.

Answer the following comprehension questions on paper.

1. What were the two horses doing? The two horses were pulling a cart piled high with jars and dishes down a hill.

2. Why did the old horse go down the hill slowly? The old horse went down the hill slowly because he did not want the cart to start rolling too fast.

3. What happened to the young horse and his cart? The young horse started going down the hill too fast so his cart started going faster and faster until the horse and cart went tumbling into a ditch and all the jars and dishes were broken.

4. Do you know what "ruts" are? Ruts are furrows or tracks worn into the dirt.

5. What did the young horse learn from the accident? The young horse learned from the accident that old horses know best after all.

6. Did you ever get into trouble because you thought you knew better than some older person? Share about your experience.

To review the long *e* vowel sound, make as many rhyming words as you can with the words *each* and *he*.

Use the provided worksheet to practice the skill of cause and effect.

Answers:

1. The <u>cart rolled down the hill</u> so fast, <u>it couldn't stop at the bottom</u>. Cause—Effect

2. <u>Due to the approaching storm</u>, <u>our picnic was cancelled</u>. Cause—Effect

3. <u>The tires went flat</u> <u>after riding over the broken glass</u>. Effect—Cause

4. <u>The older horse was wiser</u> <u>because he had lived longer</u>. Effect —Cause

5. <u>More water was added to the pool</u> <u>after the kids had been splashing about</u>. Effect—Cause

6. <u>We traveled to the mountains</u> <u>so we could snow ski</u>.   Cause
—Effect

OLD HORSES KNOW BEST, p. 15

An *effect* is what happened. A *cause* is why something happened. For example: On the hot and humid day, his ice cream cone melted quickly. The "hot and humid day" is what caused the ice cream cone to melt. "Ice cream cone melted" is the effect of the hot and humid day. In the following sentences, underline the cause and write a "C" above it, and underline the effect and write an "E" above it.

1. The cart rolled down the hill so fast, it couldn't stop at the bottom.

2. Due to the approaching storm, our picnic was cancelled.

3. The tires went flat after riding over the broken glass.

4. The older horse was wiser because he had lived longer.

5. More water was added to the pool after the kids had been splashing about.

6. We traveled to the mountains so we could snow ski.

THE MISER, p. 16

Preteach and review vocabulary: miser, hid, gold, garden, robber, treasure, empty, raised, sorrow, trouble, grief, and loss.

Answer the following comprehension questions on paper.

1. What is a miser? A miser is a person who is stingy or greedy with his possessions.

2. Where did the miser hide his gold? The miser hid his gold in a hole at the foot of a tree in his garden.

3. What happened to it? A robber dug up the gold and ran away with it.

4. What question did the neighbor ask the miser? The neighbor asked the miser if he ever used any of the gold.

5. Do you think it would do the miser as much good to look at the hole as to look at the gold? Yes, it would do the miser as much good to look at the hole as to look at the gold because all the miser ever did was look at the gold every week. He could look at the hole every week and get just as many benefits.

6. This is one of Aesop's fables; who was Aesop? What is a fable? Aesop was a Greek slave who collected fables. A fable is a very short story that teaches a useful lesson in a funny way.

7. Dramatize (act as a play) the story, using for some of the speeches the same words that people say in the fable.

There are a few long *i* words in the story: miser, night, and I. Try to list five rhyming words for each of these words.

Use the worksheet to practice the skill of writing a friendly letter.

Answer: Check for the 5 letter parts in the correct places. Also check for correct commas and capitalization.

THE MISER, p. 16

Writing a friendly letter will assist you in communication with family and friends. There are 5 basic parts to a friendly letter. The *heading* includes your address and the date. Write the heading in the upper right-hand corner, about an inch from the top of the paper. The *salutation* is a way of saying hello to the person you are writing to. It usually begins with the word *Dear* followed by the person's name. Place a comma after the person's name. Write the salutation at the left-hand margin, two lines below the heading. The *body* of the letter contains what you want to say. Begin writing on the second line after the salutation. The *closing* is a way of saying good-bye. Write your closing two lines below the body of your letter. Capitalize only the first word and follow the closing with a comma. Write your *signature* two lines below the closing. Pretend the miser has written to you expressing his troubles. Now write him a letter on notebook paper giving him friendly advice on what he should do. Be sure to include all five parts.

```
                                      HEADING


   SALUTATION,




                    BODY




                 CLOSING,

                 SIGNATURE
```

THE DOG AND THE HORSE, P. 17

Preteach and review vocabulary: farmyard, spring, fields, grain, ripening, wheat, autumn, harvest, lucky, cattle, guard, thieves, enter, plow, oats, barley, and watchdog.

Answer the following comprehension questions on paper.

1. What did the neighbors say about Stefan's farm? The neighbors always said, "Stefan has a fine farm. He is a lucky man."

2. Can you use another word instead of *autumn*? You could use the word *fall* instead of the word *autumn*.

3. Read the dog's speech to the horse.

4. Read the reply of the horse.

5. Why did the dog have nothing to say? The dog had nothing to say because he knew the horse was right.

6. Which do you think is the more helpful to the farmer, the dog or the horse? Why? Accept a choice and support for the answer.

7. What mistake did the dog make? The dog made the mistake of boasting about how important he was while forgetting how important the horse was.

On the worksheet, write a summary of the story. The long *o* sound is presented in this story in five words. See if you can find them.

Answers to long *o* words: yellow, so, no, oats, home

Answer: Accept something like this: A dog and horse, who live on the same farm, have a talk about their jobs. The dog tells the horse that the farm can get along without him because all he does is plow or draw a cart all day and sleep all night. The horse agrees that the dog keeps the cattle out of the fields of grain and guards the barns and house all night. The horse also says that if he didn't plow the fields there would be no grain to guard. This leaves the dog speechless.

THE DOG AND THE HORSE, p. 17

A summary is a short way of pulling out the main points of a story and
retelling the story in your own words. Summarize this story on
the following lines by highlighting only the main points of the
story.

_____

_____

_____

_____

_____

_____

_____

_____

_____

_____

_____

_____

THE FOX AND THE CROW, p. 18

Preteach and review vocabulary: crow, cheese, beak, fox, Madam, beautiful, feathers, voice, praise, mouth, snapping, foolish, and flatter. Answer the following comprehension questions on paper.

1. What plan had the fox for getting the cheese? The fox planned to get the cheese by telling the crow that she must have a fine voice. When the crow opened her mouth to sing, the cheese dropped to the ground, and the fox snapped it up.

2. Did the plan work well? Yes, the plan worked well because the crow was pleased by the fox's praise and opened her mouth to sing.

3. What did the crow learn when it was too late to save the cheese? When it was too late to save the cheese, the crow learned the fox was only saying nice things to get the cheese, not because he meant them.

4. Tell the story in your own words.

5. This is another of Aesop's fables; what lesson did Aesop intend to teach in it? Aesop intended to teach that you should beware of people who give false praise because their motives may not be in your best interest.

There are two words in this story with the long u sound. Locate them and then tell five other words that have a long u sound.

Answers to long u sound: beautiful and you

On the worksheet you will practice using adjectives.

Answers will vary.

THE FOX AND THE CROW, p. 18

Adjectives are words that describe nouns. Round, musical, and lofty are
   all examples of adjectives. You have just finished reading a short
   tale about a fox and a crow. Let's see how many describing words
   you can come up with to tell about the fox and the crow.

fox	crow
example: vocal	flying

THE CLOWN AND THE FARMER, p. 19

Preteach and review the following vocabulary: clown, circus, squeal, pretended, shouted, and hidden.

There are no comprehension questions for this story.

For an extension, design a colorful poster to advertise a circus coming to your town. Be sure to include the facts (who, what, when, where).

To review all the long vowel sounds, use another piece of paper and make columns for each long vowel sound. Find at least two words from this story to fit into each column. Long *u* has one word.

Answers to vowel review: long *a*—made, day, came, a; long *e*—squeal, people, he, pretended, behind; long *i*—like, I, behind; long *u*—you

Use the provided worksheet to practice comparing and contrasting.

Answers will vary.

THE CLOWN AND THE FARMER, p. 19

When you compare and contrast something, you are listing how two
   things are alike as well as how they are different. In this story,
   two main characters are mentioned. On the chart below, compare
   and contrast each character.

Clown	Both	Farmer

example:
    wearing baggy,
    puffy clothing
	men	wearing suit

WHY THE RABBIT'S TAIL IS SHORT, p. 20

Preteach and review the following vocabulary: rabbit, happened, swamp, plants, alligator, poked, afraid, trick, hundreds, leaves, family, angrily, thousands, certainly, count, bridge, sly, and jaws

Answer the following comprehension questions on paper.

1. Why did the rabbit wish to cross the swamp? The rabbit wished to cross the swamp so he could eat the juicy plants on the other side.

2. What reason did the rabbit give for thinking that the alligator was too proud to carry him across the swamp? The reason the rabbit gave for thinking that the alligator was too proud to carry him across the swamp was that the alligator could both walk and swim.

3. Find lines that show why the rabbit is called "sly." The following lines show that the rabbit is sly: "Perhaps I can get across the swamp by playing a trick upon him." "I'll count the alligators, and then you may count the rabbits." "I'll call the rabbits together some other day, when I am not so hungry."

4. Read the rabbit's boastful words after he got across the swamp.

5. What shows that the rabbit laughed too soon? It shows that the rabbit laughed too soon when one of the alligators snapped off the end of the rabbit's tail as he was boasting.

6. Tell the story in your own words.

For an extended writing lesson, write a tale explaining how a different animal got a unique characteristic. For example, you could tell how a porcupine got its quills, a leopard got its spots, or a zebra got its stripes.

Use the provided worksheet to practice antonyms and character motives.

Answers:
1. short 2. dry 3. active 4. brave 5. cool 6. enemy 7. glad 8. cry 9. evening 10. dirty (Accept other reasonable antonyms.)

1. No, the rabbit did not really want to count all the alligators because it would have been too much trouble. 2. The motive behind having the alligators line up was to make a bridge to the other side of the swamp.

WHY THE RABBIT'S TAIL IS SHORT, p. 20

Antonyms are words with opposite meanings. Hot and cold are antonyms. Write the antonyms of each of the following words.

1. long _____   2. juicy _____

3. lazy _____   4. afraid _____

5. warm _____   6. friend _____

7. angry _____   8. laugh _____

9. morning _____   10. clean _____

Why a character says or does certain things are called a character's motives. In this story, the rabbit had a certain reason for wanting the alligators to all line up in the swamp. Answer the two questions about the rabbit's motives.

1. Did the rabbit really want to count all of the alligators? Why or why not?

_____

_____

_____

2. What was the rabbit's real motive for having all the alligators line up?

_____

_____

_____

THE SIMPLETON, P. 23

Preteach and review the following vocabulary: simpleton, jingling, money, pocket, basket, rudely, sir, enough, merry, twenty, pieces, splendid, market, worth, palace, servant, present, indeed, half, keeper, reward, promise, business, farther, moments, throne, gift, Majesty, wisely, whispering, jewels, sound, beating, plenty, lad, fifty, strokes, stairs, honest, stare, wonder, treat, strangers, claimed, and aloud.

Answer the following comprehension questions on paper.

1. What is a "simpleton"? A simpleton is a person who is silly or foolish.

2. Where did Simpleton get his money? Simpleton got his money from his brothers who had sent him away from home.

3. What did he buy with it? Simpleton bought a goose with his money.

4. What did he do with the goose? Simpleton took the goose to the palace to give to the king.

5. What does Act II tell you? Act II tells how Simpleton wanted to take the goose to the king, but the first servant and second servant made Simpleton promise each of them half of his reward before they would take him to the king.

6. What does Act III tell you? Act III tells that Simpleton gave the goose to the king, and then the king offered Simpleton a reward. Simpleton asked for a beating instead of money or jewels.

7. Why did Simpleton ask the king for a "sound" beating? Simpleton asked the king for a sound beating because he was going to give his reward to the greedy servants.

8. Act the story.

For an extension to go with this play, make some simple puppets and props to help you retell the story.

Use the provided worksheet to learn about the different types of sentences found in this play.

Answers: 1. ? interrogative 2. . declarative 3. ! or . exclamatory or declarative 4. . imperative 5. ! exclamatory

Check sentences for proper identification and punctuation.

THE SIMPLETON, p. 23

There are different types of sentences. Declarative sentences make statements and end with a period. Interrogative sentences ask questions and end with a question mark. Imperative sentences give commands and end with a period. Exclamatory sentences have strong emotion or surprise and end with an exclamation mark. Identify the following sentences and put the correct punctuation on the end. Then use the provided lines to write and identify an example of each type of sentence.

1. What is in your basket ___

_____

_____

2. Simpleton walks away from the farmer ___

_____

_____

3. The king's palace is beautiful ___

_____

_____

4. Give me your hand ___

_____

_____

5. What a simpleton you must be ___

_____

_____

THE STONE-CUTTER, p. 30

Preteach and review the following vocabulary: stone-cutter, Tawara, Japan, mountain, mallet, chisel, blocks, stone, polished, builders, rich, furnishings, fairy, granted, down, carriage, snow-white, prince, umbrella, fortune, roses, droop, drooping, bowed, watered, rice, fierce, mighty, thick, cloud, pierce, strongest, rays, earth, bloomed, poured, rivers, overflowed, banks, villages, towns, sharp, shivered, and simple.

Answer the following comprehension questions on paper.

1. Why did the stone-cutter become discontented? The stone-cutter became discontented when he carried a block of stone to a rich man's house where he saw all sorts of beautiful furnishings.

2. What wish did he make? The stone-cutter wished he were rich and that he could sleep in a soft bed.

3. Who heard his wish and granted it? The fairy of the mountains heard the stone-cutter's wish and granted it.

4. Tell of other wishes the stone-cutter made. Other wishes the stone-cutter made were to be a prince, the sun, a cloud, a mountain of stone, and to be a stone-cutter.

5. Why was he discontented each time? The stone-cutter was discontented each time because he thought he was the mightiest, but each time something came along that was mightier than he was.

6. Why was Tawara happiest when he was a stone-cutter? Tawara was happiest when he was a stone-cutter because he had learned to be satisfied with who he was.

7. How would you answer Tawara's question in the last paragraph? Accept reasonable responses to Tawara's question.

Use the following worksheet to practice the skills of sequencing and using verb tenses.

Answers:
Sequencing—3, 6, 4, 2, 7, 1, 5
Verbs—1. can 2. hear 3. ask 4. stand 5. sleep 6. see 7. find 8. wish

THE STONE-CUTTER, P. 30

After reading the story two times, put the following events in order. Place a number 1 next to the first thing that happened, a number 2 next to the second thing that happened, and so on.

_____   He found that he was a prince.

_____   "I am greater than sun and cloud. I cannot be burned and I cannot be washed away."

_____   The stone-cutter wished to become the sun.

_____   The fairy turned his hut into a beautiful house.

_____   Finally, he found that he was happy as a stone-cutter.

_____   The fairy heard the stone-cutter's wishes and began to grant them.

_____   Once he turned into a cloud, Tawara began to pour down rain.

Verbs or action words can be written in many different forms. The present tense of a verb states an action that is happening now. The past tense of a verb states an action that has happened at a time in the past. Usually an –ed is added to the end of the verb to change it from the present tense to the past tense. Sometimes the verb is irregular and you do not add an –ed to the end of the verb. See if you can name the present tense to each of the following verbs.

1. _____ could   5. _____ slept

2. _____ heard   6. _____ saw

3. _____ asked   7. _____ found

4. _____ stood   8. _____ wished

THE GOLDEN FISH, p. 34

Preteach and review the following vocabulary: island, middle, success, diamonds, golden, fisherman, starve, scolded, harm, troubled, spare, oven, loaves, satisfied, awake, planning, wash tub, bade, contented, allow, stable, rate, peace, commanded, spoiled, dare, disobey, sorrowfully, garments, mild, hooks, gleam, and scales.

Answer the following comprehension questions on paper.

1. Find lines that show the fisherman was kind-hearted. The fisherman was kind-hearted because "the old man felt so sorry for the little fish that he threw him back into the sea," "the fisherman did not like to trouble his friend again so soon," "it would have pleased him greatly if his wife had been contented now," and "the old man would think of his little friend who had been so kind to him."

2. Why did his wife scold him when he returned from fishing? The fisherman's wife scolded him when he returned because he had let the fish go, and now they had nothing to eat.

3. How did the fish pay the fisherman for his kindness? The fish paid the fisherman for his kindness by giving him the things he asked of the fish.

4. What had the fisherman's wife done that made the fish think she was not fit to rule others? The fisherman's wife kept making her husband ask for more things, and she became spoiled. The fish said she could not rule herself so she was not fit to rule others.

5. Why was the fisherman glad when the palace became a hut again? The fisherman was glad when the palace became a hut again because his wife was now quiet and mild and much easier to live with than she had been before.

6. Tell the story in your own words.

For an extension, use the worksheet to do your creative writing. To review the short *a* vowels, see if you can find 11 short *a* words in the first three paragraphs of this story.

Answers: short *a* words—an, island, man, had, many, any, last, caught, small, back, am

THE GOLDEN FISH, P. 34

Suppose you caught a fish and released it. The fish was so grateful he
told you he would help make your greatest wish come true. You
were excited and went home to think about the best thing you
could possibly hope for. Later that day, you went down to the sea
and called upon the grateful fish. Write what you would tell him
on the lines below.

_____

_____

_____

_____

_____

_____

_____

_____

_____

_____

_____

_____

BROTHER FOX'S TAR BABY, P. 40

Preteach and review the following vocabulary: brother, trotting, suddenly, boughs, edge, afternoon, tar, steals, sticky, tongue, strikes, rage, shouting, teeth, screaming, butt, woolly, bottom, dancing, happens, people, roast, branches, firewood, squirming, whiskers, scorching, hurrah, scornfully, and armful.

Answer the following comprehension questions on paper.

1. What does Act I tell you about Brother Rabbit? Act I tells you that Brother Rabbit does not like to be hot.

2. Why did Brother Fox want to catch Brother Rabbit? Brother Fox wanted to catch Brother Rabbit because he did not like people sneaking into his house.

3. What plan did Brother Fox make for catching him? Brother Fox's plan for catching Brother Rabbit was to leave a tar baby in the path near his house. When Brother Rabbit touched the tar baby, he would be stuck there, and Brother Fox was going to roast him for dinner.

4. Tell how Brother Rabbit got caught. Brother Rabbit got caught when he came across the tar baby. When the tar baby wouldn't talk to him, he became angry. He hit the tar baby, and his hand got stuck. He continued to hit the tar baby until his hands, feet, and head were stuck.

5. How did Brother Rabbit get free? Brother Fox built a fire to roast him. The fire melted the tar, and Brother Rabbit escaped.

6. Dramatize the story.

You have now read all the stories in the first part of the book.

Answer the questions to follow. Which story did you think was the funniest? Which story taught the best lesson?

Answers: 1. it is 2. let's 3. do not 4. I'll 5. I'd 6. you will 7. could not 8. we'll 9. shouldn't 10. I have

BROTHER FOX'S TAR BABY, p. 40

Contractions are words that are made up of two separate words. When you choose to use a contraction, some letters of the second word are dropped, and an apostrophe is put in its place. For example: cannot is changed to can't. Fill in the appropriate contraction or two words that make up that contraction.

1. it's   _____ _____

2. _____ let us

3. don't   _____ _____

4. _____ I will

5. _____ I would

6. you'll   _____ _____

7. couldn't   _____ _____

8. _____ we will

9. _____ should not

10. I've   _____ _____

THE BROWNIE OF BLEDNOCK, p. 47

Preteach and review the following vocabulary: brownie, Blednock, frightened, doorsteps, dooryards, humming, creature, wee, bright, beard, Aiken-Drum, hooted, Duncan, olden, harmless, treat, brave, crowded, twinkle, Idle Tom, wages, broth, cradles, complained, stormy, bundle, scrubbed, glimpse, visitor, heap, worn, sewed, pressed, stitch, obliged, and deeds.

Answer the following comprehension questions on paper.

1. Why were the people frightened at the wee man? The people were frightened at the wee man because they had never seen anyone who looked so strange.

2. Can you repeat the song that he sang as he went up the street? "Oh, my name is Aiken-Drum, And to do your work I've come, A bite to eat, a bed on hay, You may give; but nothing pay."

3. What was Granny Duncan's advice? What did she mean by saying, "Handsome is, as handsome does"? Granny Duncan's advice was to take baby Meg to see the strange man. If the baby liked him, it meant he was a harmless brownie. When Granny Duncan said, "Handsome is, as handsome does," she meant that you should judge a person by his deeds, not by his appearance.

4. What were some of the good deeds Aiken-Drum did? Some of the good deeds Aiken-Drum did were singing babies to sleep, tidying houses, helping with butter that would not churn or bread that would not rise, gathering the sheep on a stormy night, carrying the heavy bundle of a tired man, and safely stacking the grain.

5. Why could he not stay in the village? Aiken-Drum could not stay in the village because brownies love to work, but they will not work for pay. A poor woman forgot this and made him a coat. When he found the coat, he had to go away.

6. What strange saying of Aiken-Drum's did the people remember? The people remembered Aiken-Drum's saying "He serves himself best, who serves others most."

7. Tell the story, following this outline: (a) The wee man comes to town, (b) Granny Duncan's advice, (c) The brownie's good deeds, (d) Why Aiken-Drum left Blednock.

8. Use another word for *wages, tidy, glimpse, obliged,* and

deeds. Another word for *wages* is *pay*, for *tidy* is *clean* or *neat*, for *glimpse* is *a quick look*, for *obliged* is *required*, and for *deeds* is *acts*.

Use the following worksheet for practice with identifying main parts of the story from the beginning, middle, and end. There is a lesson on predicting outcomes, too.

Answers: Responses will vary.

THE BROWNIE OF BLEDNOCK, P. 47

Find the main parts from the beginning, middle, and end of the story. Use the given format to help you with this skill.

In the beginning of the story _____

_____

_____.

In the middle _____

_____

_____.

At the end of the story _____

_____

_____.

Predicting outcomes is a skill where you tell what you think is going to happen next in a story. You use clues from the story to help you make your prediction. Predict what you think the people of Blednock would do if a brownie came into their town again.

_____

_____

_____

_____

_____

THE FAIRIES, p. 55

Preteach and review the following vocabulary: fairies, airy, mountain, rushy, glen, folk, trooping, shore, crispy, sea-foam, reeds, watchdogs, craggy, mosses, bare, thorn, spite, and sharpest.

Answer the following comprehension questions on paper.

1. What does the first stanza tell you about the fairies? The first stanza tells you that the fairies are small, good folk who troop together, and they wear green jackets, red caps, and a white owl's feather.

2. Where do some of them make their home? Some of them make their home along the rocky shore, in the reeds of the black mountain lake, or by the craggy hillside.

3. What does the poet tell you of the fairies' watchdogs? The poet tells you that the fairies use frogs who are awake all night as their watchdogs.

4. What would happen to anyone who dug up the thorn trees? Anyone who dared to dig up the thorn trees would find the sharpest thorns in his or her bed that night.

5. Read aloud the stanza that you like best.

6. Why is the mountain called "airy"? The mountain is called airy because the weather is often cooler and breezier on a mountain than on the land surrounding it.

Use the worksheet for a practice in writing couplets in poetry. For a short *e* review, see if you can find eight words in the poem with the short *e* sound.

Answers to short *e* words: glen, men, red, feather, here, there, them, bed

Answers will vary.

THE FAIRIES, p. 55

This poem is written by using couplets. Couplets are two rhyming lines, one right after the other, with the same number of syllables and stresses. Be creative and write a couplet to go with each category.

Your favorite animal

_____

_____

_____

_____

Summer vacation

_____

_____

_____

_____

HOW DOUGHNUTS CAME TO BE MADE, p. 57

Preteach and review the following vocabulary: doughnuts, currants, frosting, pastry, exactly, sugar, lemon, strawberry, three-cornered, raspberry, tarts, oranges, whipped cream, spice-cake, china, oyster, quail, potatoes, gravy, mince, turnover, saucer, macaroons, dainties, noticed, delicious, marry, preacher, dough, fat, perfectly, quarreling, and wedding.

Answer the following comprehension questions on paper.

1. Tell how the little cook looked. The little cook had dark eyes, pink cheeks, white skin, and hair the color of brown sugar. He wore a snowy cap and apron and always had a wooden spoon hanging from his belt.

2. What did he cook for the fairy's dinner? The little cook made turtle soup, oyster patties, quail on toast, and mashed potatoes and gravy. For dessert, he served the fairy a turnover and a tart, a glass of orange jelly, a saucer of ice cream, and some macaroons.

3. How did the fairy prove that she was a good cook? The fairy proved that she was a good cook by noticing that the piece of toast under the quail was darker on one side than on the other.

4. How did the little cook get a wedding ring? The little cook got a wedding ring by patting flat a little ball of dough. Then, he stuck the fairy's finger through the middle then dropped it into a pan of hot fat.

5. Tell the story in your own words.

Use the worksheet to learn about similes.

Answers will vary.

HOW DOUGHNUTS CAME TO BE MADE, P. 57

Similes are phrases used to add a special spark in your writing. Similes compare two things using the words like or as. In your story, there are two similes located in the first paragraph: "cheeks as pink as his best frosting" and "skin as white as the finest pastry flour." By using those phrases, the writer paints a clear picture that is much more vivid to the reader. Complete the following similes with your own creative words.

1. **His stomach was as big as** _____.

2. **Mary's hair was like** _____.

3. **Dad's car was as** _____ **as** _____.

4. **The night was like a** _____.

5. **The stars were as** _____ **as** _____.

6. **The dog's tongue was as** _____ **as** _____.

Now select your favorite simile and draw an illustration in the box.

THE FAIRY SHOES, p. 61

Preteach and review the following vocabulary: country, christening, godmother, invited, splendid, parcel, leather, copper, pinch, loiters, errand, prompt, obedient, petted, spoiled, willful, truant, blackened, polished, stretch, marsh-marigolds, scramble, strangely, ankles, jerked, cluster, troublesome, wading, stump, handkerchief, lesson, punishment, and heeded.

Answer the following comprehension questions on paper.

1. What was the fairy godmother's gift? The fairy godmother's gift was a small pair of leather shoes with copper tips.

2. Why were the fairy shoes wonderful? The fairy shoes were wonderful because they would never wear out, and the feet wearing them could not go wrong.

3. What happened to Tim's brothers when they wore the fairy shoes? When Tim's brothers wore the fairy shoes, they learned to be prompt and obedient.

4. Why did Tim's mother make him wear them? Tim's mother made him wear the shoes because Tim was truant from school and late for dinner so many times.

5. What good plan did Tim discover that his brothers had not thought of? Tim's good plan that his brothers had not thought of was to leave the fairy shoes in the mud.

6. What did Tim find when he reached his school? When Tim reached his school, he found the fairy shoes waiting for him.

7. Use another word for *parcel* and *cluster*. Another word for *parcel* is *package* and for *cluster* is *bunch*.

8. Tell the story in your own words.

Use the worksheet to learn more about apostrophes.

To review the short *i* vowel sound, find at least five words from the first page of your story with the short *i* sound.

Answers to short *i* words: little, is , rich, bring, string, it, tips

Answers: 1. Susan's turn 2. my brother's bike 3. sun's rays 4. kitten's paws

A fairy gave a child some special shoes. These shoes could help her run very fast. What do you think the child did first? That is right! She tried racing her brother. Even though her brother's speed was fast, the girl's shoes allowed her to zip right past him. He was amazed! How did you do that?

THE FAIRY SHOES, P. 61

You've already seen how apostrophes can be used in contractions. Apostrophes can also be used to show that an item belongs to someone or something. It is used to show possession. In your story, possession is shown throughout. For example, the "baby's mother" tells us that the mother belongs to the baby. Add the apostrophe to each of the following to show possession.

Ex. Tim—left arm   Tim's left arm

1. Susan—turn   _____

2. my brother—bike   _____

3. sun—rays   _____

4. kitten—paws   _____

Now read the following paragraph and correct it by adding punctuation where needed. There are missing apostrophes, commas, periods, quotation marks, and question marks.

A fairy gave a child some special shoes These shoes could help her run very fast What do you think the child did first That is right She tried racing her brother Even though her brothers speed was fast the girls shoes allowed her to zip right past him He was amazed How did you do that

48

BROWNIES, p. 67

Preteach and review the following vocabulary: hobgoblins, dwarfs, active, shy, churn, speck, tidy, clear, overnight, tailor, thoughtless, midnight, surer, faint, afterwards, dozen, boiling, cradle, footstep, scampered, although, ashamed, scolded, fretful, order, neatest, stitched, brass, daybreak, scuffling, skipping, promise, and dustpan.

Answer the following comprehension questions on paper.

1. What kind of boys were Johnnie and Tommy? Johnnie and Tommy were idle and lazy boys.

2. What did Tommy dream? Tommy dreamed that he spoke to an owl who told him to look in the pond to see a brownie. When he looked in the water, he saw himself and decided he was a brownie.

3. Read lines that tell what the boys decided to do, after Tommy had told Johnnie about his dream. "Let us play that we really are brownies, Johnnie, even if we are not. Let us do the housework, and be like the brownies that grandmother told us about. It will be great fun to surprise Father and Grandmother. We will keep out of sight, and tell about it afterwards. Oh, do come! It will be such fun!"

4. Did the boys really help their father by their work? Yes, the work the boys did really helped their father because it gave him more time to work.

5. Who became the best brownie of all after a while? The baby sister grew up to be the best brownie of them all.

Practice using commas on the provided worksheet.

Answers:

1. Brandon had to clean his room, take out the trash, and put away his clothes before going outside with Bobby.

2. While mixing the dough, make sure you add the correct amount of sugar, flour, butter, and eggs.

3. Cars, planes, trains, submarines, and mopeds are all forms of transportation.

4. To take care of a pet you must bathe it, feed it, give it water, and give it attention.

5. I like playing baseball because I can hit the ball, catch pop flies, run the bases, and cheer with my friends.

BROWNIES, p. 67

Commas can be used for many different purposes. One way commas are used is to separate words in a series. Here is an example from your story: "…this brownie would get up, sweep the room, set the table, milk the cow, churn the cream, bring the water, and scrub the floors." In the following sentences, add commas where needed.

1. Brandon had to clean his room take out the trash and put away his clothes before going outside with Bobby.

2. While mixing the dough, make sure you add the correct amount of sugar flour butter and eggs.

3. Cars planes trains submarines and mopeds are all forms of transportation.

4. To take care of a pet you must bathe it feed it give it water and give it attention.

5. I like playing baseball because I can hit the ball catch pop flies run the bases and cheer with my friends.

THE JUMBLIES, p. 75

Preteach and review the following vocabulary: Jumblies, sieve, spite, morn, pea-green, veil, tobacco-pipe, mast, voyage, extremely, Western, silvery, jackdaws, lollipop, ring-bo-ree, stilton cheese, forty, twenty, Torrible Zone, Chankly Bore, health, dumplings, and yeast.

Answer the following comprehension questions on paper.

1. What tells you that this is a nonsense poem? This is a nonsense poem because you could not float in a sieve.

2. The poet, Edward Lear, "makes up" several nonsense words just for fun; what are some of these made-up words? Some of the words Edward Lear made up are ring-bo-ree, Torrible Zone, and Chankly Bore.

3. Which stanza gave you the best laugh?

4. Why would a sieve not make a good boat? A sieve would not make a good boat because it has lots of holes in it.

5. Use another word for *extremely* and *voyage*. Another word for *extremely* is *exceptionally* and for *voyage* is *journey*.

Use the worksheet to practice your descriptive writing skills.

For the phonics practice, brainstorm more words that have the same short *o* sound as morn and stormy.

Answers: Accept reasonable descriptive writing.

THE JUMBLIES, p. 75

Who do you think the Jumblies are? Use the clues from this piece of poetry to write a story about the Jumblies. Be sure to include what they look like, where they're from, what they're doing, and why they might be traveling.

_____

_____

_____

_____

_____

_____

_____

_____

_____

_____

_____

_____

_____

THE SKYLARK'S SPURS, p. 77

Preteach and review the following vocabulary: skylark, habit, fault, sigh, replied, mate, breast, quarrelsome, spurs, chirping, good-tempered, praise, trembling, certainly, pity, hedge, clasped, and silence.

Answer the following comprehension questions on paper.

1. What showed that the fairy was unkind? The fairy was shown to be unkind because she found fault with everybody.

2. What did the fairy say the skylark did with his spurs? The fairy said that the skylark used his spurs for fighting.

3. How did the grasshopper comfort the skylark? The grasshopper comforted the skylark by saying to him that he would tell everyone that the skylark was a very good-tempered bird.

4. How did the skylark win a mate? The skylark won a mate by singing beautifully.

5. Where do larks make their nests? Larks make their nests in the grass.

6. What did the skylark find his spurs were for? The skylark found that his spurs were for carrying the eggs.

7. Tell the story in your own words.

The skill is a practice on compound words.

For an extension, look up information on a computer or in an encyclopedia about the skylark or any other bird of interest.

Now answer the section questions that relate to the selections in the Brownies and Fairies group. Which story in this group did you like best? Why do you think the brownies are the nicest of the little folks who live in the land of "Make-Believe"?

Answers: The six compound words are skylark, everybody, everyone, himself, anyway, and quarrelsome.

THE SKYLARK'S SPURS, p. 77

Compound words are words that are made when two or more words are linked together. This story contains many compound words. For example, grasshopper, is a compound word because *grass* and *hopper* are two separate words that form this compound word. From the list of 12 words, see if you can select the six that are compound words.

comfort   skylark   unhappy   moment   everyone   anyway

frighten   perhaps   everybody   almost   himself   quarrelsome

_____   _____

_____   _____

_____   _____

FAREWELL TO THE FARM p. 85

Preteach and review the following vocabulary: farewell, coach, eager, mounting, chorus, stable, fare, evermore, ladder, hayloft, cobwebs, cling, crack, whip, and woody.

Answer the following comprehension questions on paper.

1. What tells you that the "eager" children are in the country? Why were they "eager"? The eager children are in the country because the things they say farewell to are found on a farm in the country. They are probably eager to go to the city to attend school.

2. What do you see in the picture on page 85? The picture on page 85 shows children climbing into a carriage and waving good-bye to a farmer.

3. Where do you think the children are going? The children are probably going into the city to attend school.

4. What does the picture on page 86 suggest to you? The picture on page 86 suggests that the children are going to start school because it pictures school materials.

5. What does the poet mean by saying "the trees and houses smaller grow"? The poet means that the trees and houses appear to be growing smaller because the children are moving farther away from them.

Use the worksheet for more practice with compound words.

Possible answers are good-for-nothing, good-hearted, good-humored, good-looking, good-natured, good-neighbor, and good-tempered.

FAREWELL TO THE FARM, p. 85

You have just learned that a compound word is made up of two or more words. A hyphen is used to make some compound words. For example, good-bye is a word that uses a hyphen. There are many other compound words that begin with good. Brainstorm or look in the dictionary to find five more compound words that begin with *good* and have a hyphen. Use each word in a sentence.

1. _____

_____

2. _____

_____

3. _____

_____

4. _____

_____

5. _____

_____

A GOOD PLAY, p. 87

Preteach and review the following vocabulary: stairs, sofa, pillows, billows, several, nursery, slice, enough, till, and knee.

Answer the following comprehension questions on paper.

1. Where was the ship built? The ship was built on the stairs.

2. What did the children take with them to eat? The children took an apple and a slice of cake with them to eat.

3. What word tells that they were to sail on big waves? The word *billows* tells that the children were to sail on big waves.

4. How long did they sail? Who was in the boat? The children sailed for days and days. The narrator and Tom sailed in the boat.

5. Who can read the poem so as to make us see the sailing party?

6. Who wrote this poem? What other poems by the same writer have you read? This poem was written by Robert Louis Stevenson, who also wrote "Farewell to the Farm."

Use the worksheet to practice poetry writing.

Answers: Accept correct format for the fourth stanza.

A GOOD PLAY, p. 87

A stanza is a division of a poem in how the lines are arranged together.
This poem has three stanzas. You will notice that the first and
third stanza each have four lines. The second stanza has six lines.
Notice the rhyming pattern in each stanza. Follow the format in
the second stanza to write a fourth stanza to the poem.

_____

_____

_____

_____

_____

_____

_____

_____

_____

_____

_____

_____

THE PRINCESS WHO NEVER LAUGHED, p. 88

Preteach and review the following vocabulary: roadside, stroke, moment, struck, blow, cried, eagerly, plain, gladly, roots, worth, disappeared, thumb, greedy, intended, prisoner, position, glued, amusing, troubled, precious, and wealth.

Answer the following comprehension questions on paper.

1. How did the first son treat the old man who asked him for food? How did the second son treat him? The third son? When the old man asked the first and second sons for food, they were unkind and refused to give him any of their food. However, the third son was happy to share with the old man.

2. What happened to each of them? The first and second sons cut themselves with the ax. The third son was rewarded for his kindness.

3. How was the third son rewarded for his kindness? The third son was rewarded for his kindness when the little man told him which tree to cut down so that the third son would find a goose with golden feathers at the roots, which led to the third son getting to marry the princess and becoming a great prince.

4. Tell the story in your own words.

To learn about superlatives when making comparisons, use the worksheet.

Our final vowel sound is the short *u* sound. It is found in the words *cut* and *lunch*. Think of at least ten more words with the short *u* sound.

Answers: 1. younger 2. richest 3. oldest 4. larger 5. smarter Accept reasonable sentences.

THE PRINCESS WHO NEVER LAUGHED, P. 88

You have learned that adjectives are words that describe nouns. When we make comparisons between nouns we use superlatives. When comparing two nouns, use an adjective form with –er. When comparing three or more nouns, use an adjective form with –est. For example, Saturn is larger than Uranus. Jupiter is the largest planet of all. In the following sentences use the correct form of the adjective given.

1. Sam is _____ than his sister. (young)

2. The king is the _____ man in the land. (rich)

3. We visited the _____ castle in England. (old)

4. The sun is _____ than the moon. (large)

5. Sarah is _____ than her sister. (smart)

Now use each of these three words in comparative sentences: youngest, older, and richer.

_____

_____

_____

_____

_____

_____

THE BOY AND HIS CAP, p. 93

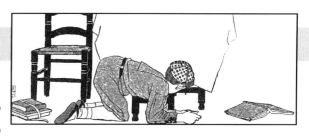

Preteach and review the following vocabulary: squint, finest, print, spy, escape, fairly, snap, strength, wasted, and chap.

There are no comprehension questions for this poem.

Use the provided worksheet for a practice with antonyms.

Answers: 1. dull 2. day 3. capture 4. cloudy 5. white 6. lose 7. girl 8. dull 9. found 10. always Accept other reasonable responses.

THE BOY AND HIS CAP, p. 93

Antonyms are words that are opposites of each other. Fill in the blank with the word that means the opposite of the listed word.

1. bright _____

2. night _____

3. escape _____

4. clear _____

5. black _____

6. find _____

7. boy _____

8. sharp _____

9. lost _____

10. never _____

Now think of 5 other antonym pairs on your own.

_____   _____

_____   _____

_____   _____

_____   _____

_____   _____

THE GOLDEN PEARS, p. 94

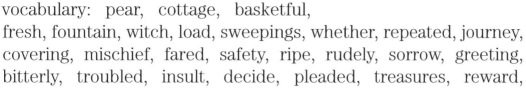

Preteach and review the following vocabulary: pear, cottage, basketful, fresh, fountain, witch, load, sweepings, whether, repeated, journey, covering, mischief, fared, safety, ripe, rudely, sorrow, greeting, bitterly, troubled, insult, decide, pleaded, treasures, reward, commanded, charge, and fortune.

Answer the following comprehension questions on paper.

1. On what errand was the oldest son sent? The oldest son was sent to deliver his father's fine pears to the king.

2. How did he answer the witch that he met? The oldest son lied to the witch and told her he only had road sweepings in his basket.

3. What happened when he reached the palace? When the oldest son reached the palace, he gave his basket to the king who found only road sweepings. The oldest son was thrown into prison.

4. How did the second son answer the witch? The second son answered the witch by telling her he only had pigs' food in the basket.

5. What happened to the second son? The second son was also sent to prison because the king found pigs' food in the basket instead of pears.

6. What did the youngest son reply to the witch's question? The youngest son told the witch that he had ripe, yellow pears in his basket.

7. What did the witch do to help the youngest son? The witch helped the youngest son by replacing his pears with ones of gold.

8. How did the king reward the boy? The king rewarded the boy by promising him he could have whatever he asked.

9. Find what the king said about telling the truth. "It is always best to tell the truth."

10. How did the king help the boy's father? The king helped the boy's father by giving him charge of the gardens about the palace.

Use the worksheet for more sequencing practice.

Answers: 1, 5, 10, 2, 9, 6, 3, 8, 4, 7

THE GOLDEN PEARS, p. 94

After reading this story, sequence the following events in the order in which they happened. The first one has been labeled for you.

<u> 1 </u>   A man and his sons owned a fine pear tree.

_____   The middle brother went to see how his oldest brother fared with the king.

_____   The poor man and his sons moved to the palace and took care of the gardens.

_____   The poor man sent his oldest son to the king with a basket of pears.

_____   The king tells the two older sons that it is always better to tell the truth.

_____   The middle brother joined his brother in jail because he, too, had not brought pears to the king.

_____   On the way to the king, the oldest son met a witch and told her he had road sweepings in his basket.

_____   The king's daughter told her father that the young boy brought pears fit for a king.

_____   The oldest son was put in jail by the king.

_____   The witch changed the polite, young boy's pears into shiny gold pears.

ONLY ONE MOTHER, P. 102

Preteach and review the following vocabulary: hundreds, shore, weather, dewdrops, greet, dawn, and wide.

There are no comprehension questions for this poem.

Use the following worksheet to interview your mother.

Answers will vary.

Only One Mother, p. 102

After reading this poem, take time to interview your mother. Ask her questions about her birth and early childhood. Some questions you may want to ask are below. Include your own questions and her answers.

1. Where were you born?   _____

_____

2. When were you born?   _____

3. How much did you weigh, and how long were you at birth?   _____

_____

4. What was your favorite toy?   _____

_____

5. How many brothers and sisters do you have?   _____

6. _____

_____

7. _____

_____

8. _____

_____

9. _____

_____

WHICH LOVED BEST?, P. 103

Preteach and review the following vocabulary: forgetting, Nell, tongue, teased, pouted, rejoiced, Fan, busy, and guessed.

Answer the following comprehension questions on paper.

1. What did John love more than he loved his mother? John loved playing on the garden swing more than he loved his mother.

2. What did Nell love more than she loved her mother? Nell loved to tease and pout more than she loved her mother.

3. How did Fan show that she really loved her mother? Fan showed that she really loved her mother by rocking the baby, sweeping the floor, and dusting the room. She showed she loved her mother by being helpful and cheerful.

4. How do you think the mother knew which loved her best? The mother knew who loved her best by each child's actions.

Use the following worksheet to do a comparison between you and your mother.

For an extension, write your comparisons in paragraph form. The first paragraph should be an introduction to what you are writing about. The second paragraph should be the information on your mother. Your information will be written in the third paragraph. Things that you have in common will be in the fourth paragraph. In the final paragraph, write a conclusion about your information. Remember to indent each paragraph and write in complete sentences.

Answers will vary.

WHICH LOVED BEST?, p. 103

Refer back to the questions you asked your mother from the previous
story. Answer those same questions yourself. Now compare and
contrast the information about your mother with your information
on the chart below.

Mother	both	me
_____	_____	_____
_____	_____	_____
_____	_____	_____
_____	_____	_____
_____	_____	_____
_____	_____	_____
_____	_____	_____

IRENE THE IDLE, p. 104

Preteach and review the following vocabulary: Irene, idle, leading, dainty, parlor, kitchen, advice, alright, brushes, dusters, wandered, delight, mistress, nearly, speechless, whiff, wood-box, kindling, crossly, proper, shrill, pantry, presently, delightful, swift, glanced, demanded, sternly, stammered, struggle, tasks, arose, crowding, seized, contented, earnest, furniture, wound, obeyed, scrambled, companions, ought, faithful, shudder, managed, overcome, prick, cured, and idleness.

Answer the following comprehension questions on paper.

1. What words of advice did the fairy give to Irene? The fairy's words of advice to Irene were "Be up with the sun, get your work done; keep the stove bright and fire alight. Here are the brushes, here are the brooms; Here are the dusters for dusting the rooms."

2. What requests did the fire, the woodbox, the floor, the cup, and the dishes make? The fire requested that Irene give it more wood, while the woodbox asked her to put down its cover. The floor needed to be swept. The cup requested that Irene hang it up, and the dishes asked to be washed.

3. What was Irene's excuse to the fairy for the disorder of the house? Irene's excuse to the fairy for the disorder of the house was that she left things so she could do them all at once.

4. Read the fairy's reply. "Left them to do all at once! You can do only one thing at a time, whenever you begin. Did they not ask to be done?"

5. What did Irene find that she must do? Irene found that she must do one thing at a time.

6. Why was Irene's birthday such a happy one? Irene's birthday was such a happy one because she had learned her lesson about being idle.

Use the provided worksheet to explore the author's purpose in this story.

For an artistic extension, illustrate one of the rooms in this magical cottage. Be sure to include the talking objects that lived there with Irene.

Answers: Answers will vary, but check for understanding that this story was mostly written to persuade. There are entertaining elements too, but not much of the informative element.

IRENE THE IDLE, p. 104

Authors write for many purposes. They could be writing to entertain the reader. They might be writing to inform the reader on a certain topic. Another purpose authors write for is to persuade the reader. Sometimes an author includes a few of these elements into his or her writing. Answer the following questions about the author's purpose in this particular story.

1. What do you think the author's purpose was in writing this story?

_____

_____

2. What ways might this story be entertaining?

_____

_____

3. What ways might this story be persuasive?

_____

_____

4. Which element is the least shown in the purpose of this story?

_____

_____

SUPPOSE, p. 115

Preteach and review the following vocabulary: suppose, pleasanter, joke, 'twas, scold, fret, dunce, nobler, temper, creation, altered, and bravest.

Answer the following comprehension questions on paper.

1. In the first stanza, what advice does the poet give? In the second stanza? In the third? In the fourth? In the fifth? In the first stanza, the advice the poet gives is to treat mishaps as a joke. In the second stanza, the advice is to smile instead of pout. In the third stanza, the advice is to work in earnest instead of waiting. In the fourth stanza, the advice is to be thankful. In the fifth stanza, the advice is to do the best you can.

2. Why do you think it is best always to be cheerful and sweet-tempered? It is always best to be cheerful and sweet-tempered because it is better for you to be positive, and those around you will admire your positive attitude. Pouting and fretting won't change the bad situation, so you may as well make the best of it by being cheerful.

3. What words does the poet use to speak of a fine carriage drawn by two horses? The poet uses the words, "Suppose that some boys have a horse, and some a coach and pair."

Answer these section questions now that you have completed the part of the book labeled Children. Which selection in this part of the book gave you the best laugh? Which selection gave you the best advice? Which selection did you think most interesting?

Use the worksheet for an activity with guide words from a dictionary.

Answers will vary based on the dictionary you used.

SUPPOSE, P. 115

Guide words are words located at the top of every page of a dictionary. They list the first and last words found on that page. They help you know which words fall in alphabetical order between the guide words. Use your dictionary to look up the following words. Then write the guide words found at the top of the page where you found each word.

1. scold _____ _____

2. pout _____ _____

3. suppose _____ _____

4. coach _____ _____

5. earnest _____ _____

6. temper _____ _____

7. creation _____ _____

8. alter _____ _____

9. wise _____ _____

10. plan _____ _____

GOOD NIGHT AND GOOD MORNING, p. 117

FRANCES KERR COOK

Preteach and review the following vocabulary: smoothed, rooks, lowed, bleat, foxglove, and curtsied.

There are no comprehension questions for this poem.

Homophones will be practiced on the provided worksheet.

Answers: Check for correct usage of each word and that you see proper sentence structure.

GOOD NIGHT AND GOOD MORNING, p. 117

Homophones are words that sound the same, but are spelled differently. These words also have different meanings. For example, *too* and *two* sound the same but are spelled differently and have different meanings. Listed below are six sets of homophones. Use each of these words in a sentence to show its meaning.

1. fair/fare	2. eye/I	3. see/sea
4. dear/deer	5. way/weigh	6. road/rode

1. _____

_____

2. _____

_____

3. _____

_____

4. _____

_____

5. _____

_____

6. _____

_____

ULYSSES AND THE BAG OF WINDS, p. 119

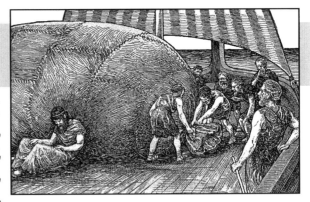

Preteach and review the following vocabulary: Ulysses, island, Greece, country, captured, against, war, joyfully, Aeolus, bronze, soundly, smooth, mountains, stormy, ox-hide, harm, chain, gentle, untie, safety, guarded, silver, fields, roaring, howling, moment, arose, and fault.

Answer the following comprehension questions on paper.

1. How long were Ulysses and his men away from home, fighting for their country? Ulysses and his men were away from home for ten long years.

2. On their way home, where did they stop to rest? On their way home, they stopped to rest at the home of a king named Aeolus, who lived on an island in the sea.

3. How did Aeolus help them? Aeolus helped them by giving Ulysses a bag of all the stormy winds to make their trip home safer.

4. Why did he leave the west wind out of the bag? The gentle west wind was left out of the bag so that they would bear Ulysses and his men safely home.

5. Who watched the bag of winds on the journey homeward? Ulysses guarded the bag of winds for nine days and nights.

6. Who untied the bag? Why? What happened? The men with Ulysses untied the bag because they thought it was filled with gold and silver. The men felt that they should get some since they helped him win the war. When the men untied the bag, out flew all the strong winds and took them far, far away.

7. Did Ulysses ever get back to his home? Yes, after many long years, Ulysses saw his island home again.

Practice telling the difference between fact and opinion on the following worksheet.

Answers: 1. fact 2. opinion 3. opinion 4. fact 5. opinion 6. fact 7. fact 8. opinion 9. opinion 10. fact

ULYSSES AND THE BAG OF WINDS, p. 119

Knowing the difference between fact and opinion is important. A fact is a detail about something that is true and can be proven. An opinion is a feeling or belief about something. Decide if each of the following statements is a fact or an opinion. Write your choice on the blank.

1. _____ The largest mammal in the world is the blue whale.

2. _____ Turtles make better pets than fish.

3. _____ Pizza is the best food to eat at a birthday party.

4. _____ French fries are made from potatoes.

5. _____ Football is more fun to watch than baseball.

6. _____ Texas is in the United States.

7. _____ Some eggs come from chickens.

8. _____ All people should learn how to row a boat.

9. _____ Dogs are smarter than pigs.

10. _____ Gold is more expensive than silver.

WHICH WIND IS BEST?, p. 122

Preteach and review the following vocabulary: whichever, doth, east, and west.

There are no comprehension questions for this poem.

Use the worksheet to learn that some words can be used as a noun or a verb.

Answers: Accept correct usage of the given words.

WHICH WIND IS BEST, p. 122

The word *wind* as it is talked about in this poem uses the short *i* sound, and is a noun. If you pronounce wind with a long *i* sound, it is a verb meaning to turn a lever. There are many other words that can be used as a noun or a verb. Use the following words as a noun in the first sentence and then as a verb in the second sentence: dance, order, part, jam, and rest.

1. _____

_____

2. _____

_____

3. _____

_____

4. _____

_____

5. _____

_____

THE STAR AND THE LILY, p. 123

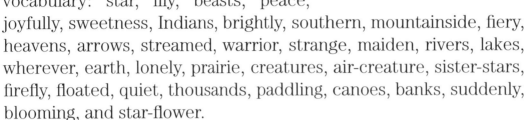

Preteach and review the following vocabulary: star, lily, beasts, peace, joyfully, sweetness, Indians, brightly, southern, mountainside, fiery, heavens, arrows, streamed, warrior, strange, maiden, rivers, lakes, wherever, earth, lonely, prairie, creatures, air-creature, sister-stars, firefly, floated, quiet, thousands, paddling, canoes, banks, suddenly, blooming, and star-flower.

Answer the following comprehension questions on paper.

1. What dream did the young warrior have? The young warrior dreamed that he climbed the mountainside to find the strange star. The star changed into a beautiful maiden who asked if she could live where she could see the children always.

2. Why did the star not like its home in the white rose on the mountainside? At the home in the white rose on the mountainside, the star was lonely, for no child came near it.

3. Why did it not like its prairie home? The star didn't like its prairie home because the little air creature flew about only at dusk, so the star never saw the children.

4. What was the little "creature of the air" that the star lived with for a while on the prairie? The "creature of the air" was a firefly.

5. Why did the star choose to live upon the lake? The star chose to live upon the lake because by day it could see children and by night the sister-stars of the sky will come to stay beside it.

6. What flower did the star become when it came to live upon the lake? What did the Indians call it? The star became a water lily when it came to live upon the lake. The Indians called it the star-flower.

Use the worksheet to learn about conjunctions.

Answers: 1. and 2. because 3. when 4. but 5. so 6. or

THE STAR AND THE LILY, P. 123

Conjunctions are words that connect other words or groups of words. The most commonly used conjunctions are and, but, or, so, because, and when. Use the conjunction that sounds best in each of the following sentences. Use each conjunction only once.

1. I ate one cookie, _____ she ate the other one.

2. We forgot our book bags _____ we were rushing.

3. Nancy washed her car _____ she came home from her trip.

4. He wanted to see you, _____ you had already left.

5. It started storming, _____ we turned off the computer.

6. I will go to a movie, _____ I will go bowling.

LITTLE PAPOOSE, p. 127

Preteach and review the following vocabulary: rock-a-by, papoose, whip-poor-will, dying, murmuring, slumbering, Manitou, and gleams.

There are no comprehension questions for this poem.

For an extension, reread the poem. Think about all the things that your mother does for you to make you feel special and keep you safe. Write her a note expressing your feelings about her and how she makes you feel.

Review the short vowel sounds with the worksheet.

Answers will vary: Short *a*—papoose, stars, warm; short *e*—nest, her, when; short *i*—river, little, his; short *o*—come, gone, robins, loves; short *u*—runs, hush, slumbering

LITTLE PAPOOSE, p. 127

Find words from this poem to fit in each category. Then finish the list with brainstormed words.

	short *a*	short *e*	short *i*	short *o*	short *u*
1.					
2.					
3.					
4.					
5.					
6.					
7.					
8.					
9.					
10.					

PEBOAN AND SEEGWUN, p. 128

Preteach the following vocabulary: Peboan, Seegwun, brooks, bare, except, whistling, wigwam, blaze, deeds, burst, arose, weak, arbutus, patches, petals, and rosy.

Answer the following comprehension questions on paper.

1. What was the old Indian doing as he sat in the wigwam? The old Indian was thinking of the great deeds he had done when he was young.

2. What "great deeds" did he say he had done? The old Indian's great deeds were turning water into ice, filling the air with snow, and making the ground hard.

3. What great deeds did the tall young man say that he could do? The tall young man said that he could melt the ice, fill the air with sunshine, and make the ground soft and warm.

4. In the morning, what became of the old man? In the morning, the old man was nowhere to be seen; he had gone.

5. Who was the old Indian? The young Indian? The old Indian was Peboan, the Winter, and the young Indian was Seegwun, the Spring.

6. What flower was seen where the old man's fire had been? The flower that was seen where the old man's fire had been was the arbutus.

7. Why is this flower said to belong both to winter and spring? The arbutus was seen to be winter with rosy petals from Peboan's fire because it loves the cold so much that it blooms while patches of snow are still upon the ground. It was seen to be spring because it is always the first flower to welcome Seegwun.

Answer the following section questions. Which of these legends did you think was the most interesting?

Commit to memory "Which Wind Is Best?"

You will review cause and effect on the following practice worksheet.

Answers: Accept reasonable causes and effects to each situation.

PEBOAN AND SEEGWUN, P. 128

Let's review cause and effect. Fill in the chart below with a possible cause or effect.

cause	effect
It started raining so	
	the cyclist scraped his knee.
When I received money for my birthday	
If you forget to clean your room	
	we made lots of money.
When I walk up the mountain	
	the birds came back.
If we stay up too late	
	my toy was broken.

A THANKSGIVING FABLE, p. 131

Preteach and review vocabulary: Thanksgiving, fable, thankfulness, mused, overheard, and declined.

Answer the following comprehension questions on paper.

1. What did the hungry cat watch on Thanksgiving morning? The hungry cat watched a little mouse on Thanksgiving morning.

2. What did the cat say? (Read the lines.) "If I ate that thankful little mouse how thankful he should be, when he has made a meal himself, to make a meal for me! Then with his thanks for having fed, and his thanks for feeding me, with all his thankfulness inside, how thankful I shall be!"

3. What did the mouse do when she heard the cat's words? Upon hearing the cat's words, the little mouse declined to stay.

4. Read the poem so as to bring out the fun of it.

5. What word does the poet use for *refused*? For *thought about* in the last stanza? The poet uses the word *declined* for *refused* and the word *mused* for *thought about*.

Use the worksheet to enjoy a writing activity.

Answers will vary. Check for correct paragraph and sentence structure.

A THANKSGIVING FABLE, p. 131

What are you thankful for? On a separate piece of paper make a list of ten things you are thankful for. Then choose one. Write about the one thing you chose. Remember paragraph one is your introduction. Paragraphs two through four each include one reason why you are thankful for your choice. Your conclusion should pull all your thoughts together in paragraph five.

_____

_____

_____

_____

_____

_____

_____

_____

_____

_____

_____

_____

LITTLE PUMPKIN'S
THANKSGIVING, P. 132

Preteach and review vocabulary: pumpkin, Peter Pumpkin Eater's patch, Frost King, sparkled, chilly, buildings, Princess Cinderella, indeed, sunbeams, napping, snuggled, beneath, jack-o'-lantern, hospital, bowing, stooped, gaily, coach, tucked, whirled, silver dollars, corners, longing, and promised.

Answer the following comprehension questions on paper.

1. What wish did the Little Wee Pumpkin make? Little Wee Pumpkin wished to make some little child very happy on Thanksgiving Day.

2. Tell how the Little Wee Pumpkin's wish came true. Cinderella came into the garden with Peter and picked Little Wee Pumpkin to take with her. She wanted to give it to a sick girl at the hospital.

3. How have you made someone happy at Thanksgiving time?

4. Tell the story in your own words.

You will practice inferences on the following worksheet.

Answers: 1. The month this story takes place in is November, because that is when Thanksgiving is. 2. The story says that Peter bows to Cinderella, so Peter may work for Cinderella. 3. No, Cinderella must not come to the pumpkin patch often because the little pumpkin was very surprised to see her.

LITTLE PUMPKIN'S THANKSGIVING, p. 132

Inferences are ways we figure out what is going on in a story. We use clues in what we are reading. For example, if we read that Maggie is going swimming, we would conclude that the time of year would be summer, because that is the season a person is most likely to go swimming. Answer the following inference questions from your story. Use the clues in the story to help you, and give your answers in complete sentences.

1. In what month does this story take place?

_____

_____

2. Why does Peter help Cinderella?

_____

_____

3. Does Cinderella come to the pumpkin patch very often?

_____

_____

A CHRISTMAS WISH, p. 137

Preteach and review the following vocabulary: Christmas, stocking, giant, meeting-house, search, jack-knife, sharp, Noah's ark, story-book, wild, tool-box, flannels, frocks, jolliest, wagon, caramels, almond, pecan, taffy, barrels, and oranges.

Answer the following comprehension questions on paper.

1. Why do you think the poet would like "a stocking made for a giant"? The poet wished for "a stocking made for a giant" because of all the toys and treats he would give to poor little girls and boys.

2. Make a list of all the toys that the poet thinks children would want. The toys the poet named were: jack-knife, doll, china set, Noah's ark, doll's cook-stove, toy wash-tub, little drum, story-book, set of blocks, and a tool-box.

3. What other things does he say that they would want? The other things the children would want are: shoes, warm things to wear, soft flannels for little frocks, stockings, coats, cloaks, caramels, candy, almonds, pecan nuts, taffy, and oranges.

4. Use another word for *search, beasts,* and *meeting-house.* Another word for *search* is *look,* for *beasts* is *wild animals,* and for *meeting-house* is *building.*

5. What words does the poet use in the second stanza to tell of dishes that were just the kind a girl would like best? The poet uses the words, "One would ask for a china set with dishes all to her mind," to describe what a girl would like best.

The provided worksheet is on drawing conclusions.

Answers: Accept reasonable responses.

A CHRISTMAS WISH, p. 137

Drawing conclusions means to take all the information you have and deciding what you think the outcome will be. Use this skill to answer the following questions. Then reflect on your best Christmas ever in the space provided.

What do you feel the writer is thinking about as he mentions all the toys?

_____

_____

What do you think the poet's Christmases were like when he was little?

_____

_____

Why does he want to have presents for all of these boys and girls?

_____

_____

How will the boys and girls feel on Christmas morning?

_____

_____

Reflect on your most memorable Christmas ever. Write a few statements describing how it was.

_____

_____

_____

GRETCHEN'S CHRISTMAS, P. 139

Preteach and review the following vocabulary: Gretchen, empty, American, harbor, Rupert, Santa Claus, boardinghouse, goodies, English, jostled, France, woolly, soldiers, splendid, march, gallop, satin, throne, shawl, porch, mild, evenly, Christmas Eve, Margaret, basketful, carols, moonbeams, pity, owner, Saint Nicholas, whispered, tenderly, homesick, and tidings.

Answer the following comprehension questions on paper.

1. Why did the empty shoes make Gretchen's heart sad? The empty shoes made Gretchen's heart sad because she thought that Rupert had forgotten her.

2. Which doll in the toy store window pleased Gretchen most? The doll that pleased Gretchen the most was a real baby doll with a look on its face as if it wanted to be loved.

3. What loving deeds did Margaret do on Christmas Eve? The loving deeds that Margaret did on Christmas Eve were to carry a basketful of toys to help Santa Claus.

4. What Christmas gift did Gretchen find when she awoke? The Christmas gift Gretchen found when she awoke was the wished-for baby doll.

Use the worksheet to explore characters' motives.

For an extension, research what Christmas traditions are celebrated in other parts of the world.

Answers: 1. Gretchen, her mother, and her father came to America to find a new home and opportunity. 2. Gretchen put her shoes outside the door in hopes that Rupert would fill them with goodies. 3. The woman in the boardinghouse felt sorry for Gretchen, so she took her window shopping. 4. Margaret wanted to help her father deliver presents because she was so happy and thankful, and she wanted to share that with others.

GRETCHEN'S CHRISTMAS, p. 139

Characters usually have reasons, or motives, for their actions. Give some ideas as to what you think the characters' motives were in this story.

1. Why had Gretchen, her mother, and her father come to America?

_____

_____

_____

2. Why did Gretchen put her shoes outside the door?

_____

_____

_____

3. Why did the woman in the boardinghouse take Gretchen window shopping?

_____

_____

_____

4. Why did Margaret want to help her father deliver presents?

_____

_____

_____

THE CHRISTMAS TREE, p. 146

Preteach and review the following vocabulary: glade, steep, skylark, evergreen, glittering, tinkling, and voices.

There are no comprehension questions for this poem.

Use the research about how another country celebrates Christmas and compare with our customs on the worksheet.

Answers will vary.

THE CHRISTMAS TREE, P. 146

Use your research findings from the last story to compare and contrast Christmas customs to those of another country. Include such details as traditional foods eaten, gift exchanges, who the gift giver is, and what the holiday means. Put your details on the following chart.

United States	_____

WHERE DO THE OLD YEARS GO?, p. 147

Preteach and review the following vocabulary: mistake, New Year, bow, and struck.

There are no comprehension questions for this poem.

Practice facts and opinions on the given worksheet.

Answers: 1. opinion 2. fact 3. fact 4. opinion 5. fact

WHERE DO THE OLD YEARS GO?, p. 147

Remember that facts are things that can be proven, and opinions are feelings or beliefs someone has about something. Identify each of the following statements as being a fact or opinion. If the statement is an opinion, tell why you think it is an opinion. Now write two facts and two opinions of your own.

1. _____ It is more fun to live where it snows.

2. _____ The new year begins as the clock strikes at midnight on December 31st.

3. _____ Many people make resolutions for the new year.

4. _____ Everybody has to stay up on New Year's Eve.

5. _____ In the United States, there are twelve months in a year.

FACT

1. _____

_____

2. _____

_____

OPINION

1. _____

_____

2. _____

_____

AN EASTER SURPRISE, P. 148

Preteach and review the following vocabulary: Easter, enjoying, flowerpot, cellar, tulips, underneath, weeds, armchair, curtain, and swaying.

Answer the following comprehension questions on paper.

1. What were the "round brown things" that Paul dug up in his mother's tulip bed? The round things that Paul dug up in his mother's tulip bed were tulip bulbs.

2. What did Paul do with them? Paul planted the tulip bulbs at a house on the corner where an old man and his wife lived.

3. Why did the little old lady think she would have no flower garden that year? The little old lady thought that she would have no flower garden that year because the old man had been ill and would not be able to plant the seeds, as he had done for years and years.

4. What happened to her flower bed that surprised her? The old woman was surprised to see tulips almost ready to bloom in her flower bed.

5. Why were the little old lady and her husband so happy when they saw the tulips? The little old lady and her husband were so happy when they saw the tulips because they knew that someone must love them, even if they were old and poor.

Answer the following questions about the Holidays section of this book. Which selection in this part told of the kindest act? Which told of the happiest times? Which gave you the best laugh?

Practice your skills of predicting outcomes in the following worksheet.

Answers will vary.

AN EASTER SURPRISE, p. 148

Predicting outcomes means using the direction of the story to lead you to the next part. If this story were to jump to the following Easter and all the characters were the same, what do you think would happen? Use the following lines to predict what you think would happen next year at Easter.

_____

_____

_____

_____

_____

_____

_____

_____

_____

_____

_____

_____

OLD APPLESEED JOHN, p. 153

Preteach and review the following vocabulary: Appleseed, village, heart, pennies, simple, core, pointed, whistling, roadsides, autumn, travelers, and juicy.

Answer the following comprehension questions on paper.

1. What plan for helping others did the kind old man make? The kind old man planned to help others by planting apple seeds.

2. What did the village people think of him? The village people thought Appleseed John was crazy.

3. What did the boys say of him? The boys said that Appleseed John was just as kind as he could be. They said they liked to play around his little hut and hear his funny stories and songs.

4. What did the old man do with the apple cores that he saved? The old man planted the apple cores in the fields and along the roadsides.

5. How did the old man's work help others in later years? The old man's work helped others in later years by providing shade in which to rest and juicy fruit to eat.

Use the following worksheet to practice cause and effect.

Answers: 1. The old man got paid for doing all kinds of jobs. effect, cause 2. When he thought of a way to help others, a smile came over his face. cause, effect. 3. The people in the village thought the old man was crazy because he wanted to be partly paid in apples. effect, cause 4. Some boys thought the old man was kind because he told funny stories and sang funny songs. effect, cause 5. Because the man saved all of his apple cores, the boys called him Appleseed John. cause, effect 6. Many year later, roadsides and fields were covered in apple trees because Appleseed John planted the cores. effect, cause

OLD APPLESEED JOHN, p. 153

An effect is *what* happened. A cause is *why* something happened. In the following sentences, underline the cause and write a "C" above it, and underline the effect and write an "E" above it.

1. The old man got paid for doing all kinds of jobs.

2. When he thought of a way to help others, a smile came over his face.

3. The people in the village thought the old man was crazy because he wanted to be partly paid in apples.

4. Some boys thought the old man was kind because he told funny stories and sang funny songs.

5. Because the man saved all of his apple cores, the boys called him Appleseed John.

6. Many year later, roadsides and fields were covered in apple trees because Appleseed John planted the cores.

COLUMBUS AND HIS SON, DIEGO, p. 158

Preteach and review the following vocabulary: Columbus, Diego, dusty, Spain, friars, convent, voyage, prove, unwilling, studying, written, Perez, Isabella, glance, common, beggars, rough, India, ocean, spices, silks, caravans, interest, messenger, cast, west, tease, Palos, terrible, monsters, swallow, mouthful, shores, shame, honor, royal, clasped, adventure, skins, and globe.

Answer the following comprehension questions on paper.

1. For what purpose did Columbus try to get ships? Columbus tried to get ships for his great voyage.

2. Why did Columbus think that he might find help at the convent? What help did he get from one of the friars? Columbus thought that he might find help in the convent because the friars spend their time reading and studying books. One of the friars helped by thinking Columbus was right and sending a message to Queen Isabella.

3. What did Columbus say he could prove? Columbus said he could prove that the world is round.

4. Who gave Columbus ships and money for the voyage? Queen Isabella gave ships and money for the voyage.

5. Where did Columbus leave his son, Diego, while he was away on the voyage? Columbus left Diego at the palace of the king of Spain.

6. How long did the other pages tease Diego? The other pages teased Diego for seven months.

7. What did one of the pages call the Atlantic Ocean? One of the pages called the Atlantic Ocean the Sea of Darkness.

8. Why was Columbus called The Mad Sailor? Columbus was called The Mad Sailor because he said that the world was round and that he could reach India by sailing west.

9. What message came from Columbus one day? Columbus sent a message that he had found the land beyond the sea.

10. What did Columbus discover? Columbus discovered the islands of the Carribbean and those souteast of North America.

11. What had Columbus proved by his voyage? Columbus proved that the world is round.

12. Use another word for *voyage, aid, page,* and *globe.*

Another word for *voyage* is *trip,* for *aid* is *help,* for *page* is *attendant,* and for *globe* is *sphere*.

Answers will vary. Check for correct sentence and paragraph formations.

COLUMBUS AND HIS SON, DIEGO, p. 158

Use whatever research materials you have access to and discover some
facts about Columbus and his voyage to the New World. Give
your facts in short note form on the lines below. For example:
Columbus left on August 1492.

1. _____

2. _____

3. _____

4. _____

5. _____

Now use the new information that you listed and condense it into a
paragraph below.

_____

_____

_____

_____

_____

_____

_____

_____

_____

THE BOY, THE BEES, AND THE BRITISH, P. 165

Preteach and review the following vocabulary: British, General Washington, piazza, Virginia, seizing, Old Bay, spare, fifteen, pleaded, French, army, plantation, clatter, hoofs, redcoats, starve, bellowing, squealing, squawking, rebels, commands, beehives, clump, instantly, flung, midst, scene, stings, plunged, neighing, helter-skelter, delayed, meantime, troops, and captured.

Answer the following comprehension questions.

1. Tell why 1781 was a hard year in Virginia. The year 1781 was a hard year in Virginia because British soldiers rode everywhere seizing all the horses and food they could find.

2. What did Jack wish to do? Jack wished to help General Washington in the fighting for our country.

3. Jack's mother told him why he had been left at home; read her words. Jack's mother told him, "You were left here to take care of me, Jack. The British have been here once already and have taken all our horses except Old Bay. They will surely come again. Would you want me to meet them alone?"

4. Who were the "redcoats"? The redcoats were the British men fighting in the war, who wore red uniforms.

5. Tell about the coming of the redcoats to the plantation. The redcoats came to take corn and food from the cellar. They drove up bellowing cattle and squealing pigs. They chased squawking chickens about the yard. They were looking for what horses they could find.

6. Why was Jack glad that he was at home? Jack was glad he was home to protect his mother and delay the redcoats.

7. What daring plan did Jack think of? How did he make the bees fight the British? Jack thought of throwing a beehive at the soldiers. The angry bees flew at the men and animals.

8. After he had thrown the beehive at the soldiers, what did he do? Jack rode off on Old Bay to tell the American soldiers where the British were.

9. Do you think Jack found a good way to help his country even though he was too young to join Washington's army? Yes, Jack's plan helped to capture four hundred British soldiers.

10. Use another word for *seizing, plantation,* and *clump.*

Another word for *seizing* is *taking,* for *plantation* is *estate,* and for *clump* is *cluster*.

The following worksheet gives you practice with writing quotations.

For a writing extension, pretend that you are Jack. Write a journal entry reflecting on the day you just experienced.

Answers:
1. Sally said, "I wish we could go to the park every day."
2. "The birds and squirrels are active today," said Mother.
3. "Can we wash the windows for you?" asked the twins.
4. Eve answered, "You forgot to give me the umbrella."
5. "Boys and girls, let us begin class," said the teacher.

THE BOY, THE BEES, AND THE BRITISH, p. 165

Quotation marks are used for setting off the exact words of a speaker from the rest of the sentence. For example: Martha asked, "Who can show me how to find information about England?" The quotation marks surround Martha's exact words. Also note the use of the comma, and the ending punctuation is enclosed in the quotation mark. Put quotation marks, commas, and punctuation in the given sentences. Use your story as a guide to proper usage.

1. Sally said I wish we could go to the park every day

2. The birds and squirrels are active today said Mother

3. Can we wash the windows for you asked the twins

4. Eve answered You forgot to give me the umbrella

5. Boys and girls, let us begin class said the teacher

WHY JIMMY MISSED THE PARADE ON WASHINGTON'S BIRTHDAY, P. 171

Preteach and review the following vocabulary: honor, boy scouts, curb, laws, anxiously, company, heroes, faded, governor, automobile, speech, president, grandly, recounted, purely, nation, banner, natal, processions, bugle, darted, rearing, stunned, unable, and disappointed.

Answer the following comprehension questions on paper.

1. In what parade were the boy scouts to take part? The boy scouts were to take part in the parade in honor of George Washington.

2. What soldiers were to be in the parade? A company of soldiers who had been fighting for France during World War One were in the parade.

3. Recite from memory the lines Jimmie had learned from Margaret Sangster's beautiful poem about George Washington.

4. Why did Jimmie miss the parade? Jimmie missed the parade because he was saving a little dog that had been struck by the hard hoofs of a frightened horse.

5. What happened at the scout meeting that night? When Jimmie entered the room for the scout meeting, the boys shouted, "Hurrah for Jimmie Preston. He's a good scout, all right!"

6. What other stories of kindness and helpfulness have you read in this book? Some other stories of kindness and helpfulness in this book are "Appleseed John," "Gretchen's Christmas," and "The Brownies," to name a few.

7. Use another word for *forming, blast, stunned,* and *crushed.* Another word for *forming* is *developing,* for *blast* is *outburst,* for *stunned* is *shocked,* and for *crushed* is *smashed.*

8. What words does the poet use for *birthday* in the lines Jimmie learned? For *spoken of*? The poet used *natal day* for *birthday* and *recounted* for *spoken of* in the lines Jimmie learned.

Have fun with word analogies in the worksheet.

Answers: 1. dead 2. bad 3. parking 4. frown 5. sing 6. pool
7. backward 8. kitten

WHY JIMMY MISSED THE PARADE ON WASHINGTON'S BIRTHDAY, p. 171

Word analogies are like puzzles. You have to figure out the relationship between the words. For example: *hot* is to *cold* as *loud* is to *soft*. Hot and cold are opposites, so you find the opposite of loud to complete the analogy. In this example: *first* is to *second* as *fifth* is to *sixth*, we are looking at the degree of something. Second is one step down from first, so we relate that sixth is one step down from fifth. Complete the following analogies.

1. *First* is to *last* as *alive* is to _____.

2. *Good* is to *better* as _____ is to *worse*.

3. *Come* is to *coming* as *park* is to _____.

4. *Happy* is to *smile* as *mad* is to _____.

5. *Poem* is to *read* as *song* is to _____.

6. *Bath* is to *tub* as *swim* is to _____.

7. *Forward* is to _____ as *north* is to *south*.

8. *Cat* is to _____ as *dog* is to *puppy*.

A LITTLE LAD OF LONG AGO, p. 176

Preteach and review the following vocabulary: lad, Little Abe, deerskin, leggings, clumsy, moccasins, bearskin, homespun, coonskin, fond, chinks, saucy, pattered, beloved, loft, shivering, crisp, spoiled, hastened, eagerly, fodder-corn, good-naturedly, ached, and faithfully.

Answer the following comprehension questions.

1. Why was little Abe called a funny-looking boy? Little Abe was called a funny-looking boy because he wore deerskin leggings, clumsy deerskin moccasins, a suit made of warm homespun cloth, and a coonskin cap with a tail hanging behind.

2. Why does the story say you would have liked him? The story says we would have liked him because of his honest, twinkling blue eyes.

3. Why was the borrowed book so precious to little Abe? The borrowed book was so precious to Abe because it was about the life of George Washington.

4. Why did the boy read the book at night, instead of in daytime? Abe read the book at night because he worked hard all day long.

5. Where did he put the book each night when he had finished reading it? Abe put the book in a small crack between the logs in the roof just above his bed.

6. What happened to the book one night? One night the book got wet through and through because of the snow.

7. What did little Abe do at once when he saw the book was spoiled? Little Abe at once took the spoiled book to the owner, his neighbor, looked him in the eye, and explained what had happened to it.

8. Do you think he acted in a manly way by going to the owner? Yes, Abe acted in a manly way because he was honest.

9. How did the boy earn the right to keep the book? Abe earned the right to keep the book by pulling fodder-corn for three days.

10. Can you give the name of the book? The name of the book was *The Life of George Washington*.

11. What did Abraham Lincoln say about this book, after he had become president of the United States? Abraham Lincoln said that

this book helped him to become president of the United States.

12. Use another word for *clumsy* and *chinks*. Another word for *clumsy* is *awkward* and for *chinks* is *caulk* or *mud*.

Use the worksheet to learn and practice using adjectives.

For an extension, compare and contrast President Abraham Lincoln to President John F. Kennedy. These two men have more in common than you might think.

Answers will vary.

A LITTLE LAD OF LONG AGO, p. 176

You have learned that adjectives are words that describe nouns. In this story, the use of adjectives helps you understand Abe's looks, book, and room. Fill in the chart with the adjectives used to describe these things.

looks	book	room
_____	_____	_____
_____	_____	_____
_____	_____	_____
_____	_____	_____
_____	_____	_____

Now use adjectives to describe these three things about you: your looks, your favorite book, and your room.

looks	book	room
_____	_____	_____
_____	_____	_____
_____	_____	_____
_____	_____	_____
_____	_____	_____

JACQUES, A RED CROSS DOG, p. 180

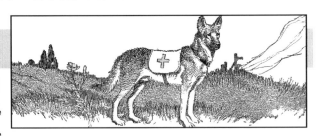

Preteach and review the following vocabulary: Jacques, shepherd, master, mistress, Francois, Nanette, Jeanne, awkward, Hugo, vegetables, cellar, straying, stew, fluttering, trained, sorrowfully, enrolled, terrier, trenches, sentinels, swift-footed, collies, battlefield, strapped, constant, gas masks, ambulance, ruts, hurled, plunge, bullets, faint, saddle pockets, chap, stretcher-bearers, stiff, lame, Cosette, and decorated.

Answer the following comprehension questions.

1. In this story who is telling of his life on the farm? Jacques, a shepherd dog, is telling this story.

2. Tell in your own words of Jacques's life on the little farm in France. Jacques lived with his master and family. In the family, there were the master, mistress, Francois, Nanette, and little Jeanne. Jacques helped to tend to Cosette, the cow. Sometimes he would hunt the rabbits that got away. Jacques walked to town every evening with Francois and sometimes carried letters from the master, who was away at war, in his mouth.

3. Tell of Jacques's training at the war-dog school. Jacques's training at the war-dog school was Red Cross work. He was trained to hunt for the wounded and dying on the battlefield, and to carry them food, drink, and medicine in little saddles that were strapped on his back. He also had to learn not to bark.

4. Tell how Jacques saved his master. Jacques saved his master by standing close by his side and letting him get what he needed from the saddle pockets. He also took a letter the master had written to one of the stretcher-bearers.

5. Jacques was "decorated" several times, that is, he was given medals or ribbons as a reward for his bravery. Did these decorations make him proud? Jacques was not proud of being decorated many times.

6. What was the only thing Jacques was proud of? The only thing Jacques was proud of was being able to save his master's life.

7. What do the words "sent to the front" mean, on page 185? The words "sent to the front" meant being sent to where the battle was being fought.

Answer the following section questions now that you have completed this part of the book. Why is it a good thing to read stories about Washington, Lincoln, and others who have helped their countries? Can you tell the class any story about some other American who helped our country? What are some of the ways in which you can show that you are a good American?

For the worksheet, summarize the story.

To extend your knowledge, find out what you can about the Red Cross organization. You may even want to volunteer for a day to support your community

JACQUES, A RED CROSS DOG, P. 180

Summarize this story in your own words. Remember that a summary is brief and includes the key points of the story. Use only the space that is provided.

_____

_____

_____

_____

_____

_____

_____

_____

_____

_____

_____

_____

_____

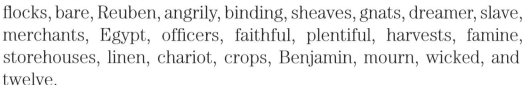

JOSEPH, THE RULER, p. 189

Preteach and review the following vocabulary: Joseph, Canaan, herds, flocks, bare, Reuben, angrily, binding, sheaves, gnats, dreamer, slave, merchants, Egypt, officers, faithful, plentiful, harvests, famine, storehouses, linen, chariot, crops, Benjamin, mourn, wicked, and twelve.

Answer the following comprehension questions on paper.

1. Which of Joseph's older brothers was kind to him? Joseph's older brother, Reuben, was kind to him.

2. Why did the others hate him? The other brothers hated Joseph because they thought that their father loved Joseph more than he loved them.

3. How did the wicked brothers get rid of Joseph? The wicked brothers got rid of Joseph by selling him as a slave to some merchants who were on their way to Egypt.

4. How did the king of Egypt show that he believed Joseph was good and wise? The king of Egypt showed that he believed Joseph was good and wise by giving him charge over all the land.

5. Why did Joseph's brothers go to Egypt? Joseph's brothers went to Egypt because they needed to buy some corn.

6. How did Joseph treat his brothers when they came to buy corn? (Wheat was known as "corn" in Joseph's time.) When Joseph's brothers came to buy corn, he treated them kindly and asked them questions about their family. They were bowing down, so they did not know it was their brother that they were talking to.

7. What made Joseph the happiest man in Egypt? Joseph was the happiest man in Egypt because his father and eleven brothers came there to live.

8. Class readings: the conversation on pages 190, 191 (five pupils); Joseph's dream, page 191 (two pupils); the meaning of the dream, pages 193, 194 (three pupils); Joseph forgives his brothers, pages 197 to 199 (eleven pupils).

Use the worksheet to practice writing captions and thinking about characters' motives.

Answers: Captions will vary; check for accuracy.

1. Joseph shared his dream with his brothers because he simply thought it was strange. 2. Jacob gave Joseph the coat of many

colors because he thought Joseph was special, and he didn't work in the pastures yet, so he wouldn't have soiled it. 3. Joseph helped his family because he loved them, and he was kind-hearted.

JOSEPH, THE RULER, p. 189

Remember that captions are phrases or sentences that describe a picture, graph, or chart. Write captions to go with each of the five pictures in the story.

1. _____

2. _____

3. _____

4. _____

5. _____

Now answer the following questions about these characters' motives.

1. **Why did Joseph want his brothers to know about his dream?**

_____

_____

2. **Why did Jacob, Joseph's father, give him the coat?**

_____

_____

3. **Why did Joseph help his family at the end of the story?**

_____

_____

DAVID, THE SINGER, p. 200

Preteach and review the following vocabulary: Bethlehem, harp, roaring, guarding, grasped, staff, firmly, instantly, robbers, sling, haste, illness, dared, spear, King Saul, troubled, enemy, battle, valley, breast, brass armor, cowards, Israel, helmet, sword, aim, victory, and express.

Answer the following comprehension questions on paper.

1. What was David's work when he was a boy? David's work when he was a boy was to take care of the sheep.

2. Tell some things that David had to do that you would like to do; what part of his work would you not like? This in an opinion, so answers will vary.

3. With what did David fight the lion? David fought the lion with his staff and his hands.

4. How did he fight the band of robbers? David fought the band of robbers with his sling, stones, and his staff.

5. How did David help King Saul? David helped King Saul by playing his harp and singing in a low, sweet voice.

6. For what is David remembered? David is remembered for the songs that he wrote.

7. Class readings: the conversation between David and his mother, pages 200, 201; the conversation on pages 203, 204, 205; the conversation on pages 206, 207, 208.

Use the following worksheet to practice fact and opinion.

Answers: 1. Opinion—different things help soothe different people. 2. Fact. 3. Opinion—size doesn't limit one person from doing as much as another person. 4. Opinion—someone may think another king was the greatest of all time. 5. Fact 6. Fact 7. Fact

NAME_____CLASS_____DATE_____

DAVID, THE SINGER, P. 200

Mark the following statements as a fact or an opinion. For the ones that are opinions, write a reason why you think it is an opinion in the spaces between each item.

1. _____ Beautiful songs help everyone feel better.

2. _____ It is the job of a shepherd to guard and take care of his sheep.

3. _____ Small, short people cannot do as much as large, tall people.

4. _____ Saul was the greatest king of all time.

5. _____ David was able to help King Saul feel better by singing and playing his harp.

6. _____ David traveled to take food to his brothers who were serving in Saul's army.

7. _____ Later, David became the king of Israel.

THE BOY AND THE SHEEP, p. 210

Preteach and review the following vocabulary: daisies, nay, nip, dewy, and wintry.

There are no comprehension questions for this poem.

Use the worksheet to review long and short vowel sounds.

Answers: 1. long *i* 2. long *i* 3. long *o* 4. long *a* 5. long *o* 6. long *e* 7. short *i* 8. short *a* 9. short *a* 10. short *a* 11. long *a*

THE BOY AND THE SHEEP, p. 210

This poem is written in couplets, which are two rhyming lines. After each pair of words, tell the vowel sound that you hear. Note the different spellings for each vowel sound.

1. why, lie   _____

2. white, night   _____

3. do, you   _____

4. nay, pray   _____

5. grows, clothes _____

6. be, me   _____

7. thing, spring   _____

8. pass, grass   _____

9. where, bare   _____

10. last, past   _____

11. away, day   _____

SAINT GEORGE AND THE DRAGON, P. 211

Preteach and review the following vocabulary: George, splendid, knights, punishing, plowman, parents, several, evil, queen, feast, refuse, throne, knelt, Una, dragon, den, boldly, prison, rescued, noble, discouraged, strength, praising, and unselfishness.

Answer the following comprehension questions on paper.

1. What story did the plowman tell George? The plowman told George the story of how a baby had been stolen from home and left in a field where he was found by a plowman. The plowman was alone so he took the baby home and named him George.

2. When George had grown tall and strong, what did he ask the queen to allow him to do? George asked the queen to allow him to do a brave deed.

3. Why did she not want to send George to fight the dragon? The queen did not want to send George to fight the dragon because he was very young, and he didn't have a horse or armor.

4. What brave deed did George do in the Wandering Wood? In the Wandering Wood, George killed a great beast that sprang at him.

5. Why was the giant able to take George prisoner? The giant was able to take George prisoner because George had laid aside his armor to drink from a spring.

6. How was George saved from the giant? Una led another knight to the giant's castle to rescue George.

7. How did the wise old man comfort him? The wise old man comforted George by telling him that he was the stolen baby, the son of a king, and that he would fight a great battle and win a great victory.

8. How has George's brave life helped other boys? George's brave life has helped other boys by inspiring them to be brave themselves.

9. Class readings: the conversation on pages 214, 215, 216 (three pupils); the wise man's words, page 217, the last three paragraphs on page 219.

Answer the following section questions. Can you tell the class of an American in World War One who was like Joseph because he saved thousands of people from starving? What other Americans do you know of who are famous because they were great soldiers, or because they helped our people in some way?

Learn about supporting details on the following worksheet.

Answers: 1. c 2. a 3. d 4. e 5. b

SAINT GEORGE AND THE DRAGON p. 211

Supporting details are the facts or ideas that are used to make or prove a point. This story contains many supporting details. See if you can match the supporting details to the point by drawing lines to connect them.

Main Points	Supporting Details
1. George told his father he wanted to be a knight.	A. Brave, strong men are needed to fight it.
2. There is so much evil in this world.	B. People will love and honor you.
3. This is the week of the great feast.	C. Your father is only a plowman.
4. George laid his armor aside.	D. The queen will not refuse anything asked.
5. You will fight a great battle.	E. He was seized by a giant.

MY CHICKADEE GUESTS, p. 220

Preteach and review the following vocabulary: chickadee, guests, study, hemp, millet, sunflower seeds, suet, whiskbroom, plump, grosbeaks, redpolls, siskin, woodpecker, interrupted, alight, shoulders, invite, sprinkled, ledge, snatching, rude, lesson, scolding, English, thread, kernel, nervous, and welcome.

Answer the following comprehension questions on paper.

1. Who was talking in this story? The man that lives in the house is telling the story.

2. How do you know that the author loves birds? You can tell the author loves birds because he takes great care to feed them in several places and even whisks away the snow that covers the food.

3. Which of the birds mentioned in this story have you seen? The birds mentioned in the story are pine grosbeaks, redpolls, a sisken, blue jays, a woodpecker, and chickadees.

4. Tell in your own words about the author's five chickadee guests at breakfast. The author wanted the five chickadees to join him inside for breakfast. The chickadees would pick up the nuts and fly out the window to eat them. Thinking that it was rude, the author sewed the nuts with a stitch to the tablecloth. Soon the chickadees, one by one, came in and ate the nuts at the table.

5. Listen while a good reader reads the story aloud.

6. Use another word for *ledge* and *certainly*. Another word for *ledge* is *ridge,* and another word for *certainly* is *surely.*

Use the worksheet for more practice with present and past tense verbs.

For an extension, write a vertical poem using the word *chickadee.* Each letter in the word begins the next line of the poem, and the first word on the line must start with that letter.

Answers: 1. were 2. fill 3. acted 4. flew 5. sprinkled 6. settle 7. invited 8. hopped 9. make 10. spoke

MY CHICKADEE GUESTS, p. 220

The present tense of a verb states an action that is happening now. The past tense of a verb states an action that has happened at a time in the past. Most times an –ed is added to the end of the verb to change it from the present tense to the past tense. Sometimes the verb is irregular, and you do not add an –ed to the end of the verb. Supply the missing verb in the lines below.

1. are   _____

2. _____ filled

3. act   _____

4. fly   _____

5. sprinkle   _____

6. _____ settled

7. invite   _____

8. hop   _____

9. _____ made

10. speak   _____

CALLING THE VIOLET, p. 225

Preteach and review the following vocabulary: mossy, shiver, slender, reeds, sigh, flutter, whisper, pine-boughs, and yon.

There are no comprehension questions for this poem.

Review guide words on the following worksheet.

Answers will vary according to your dictionary.

CALLING THE VIOLET, p. 225

Remember that guide words are words located at the top of every page of a dictionary. They list the first and last words found on that page. Use your dictionary to look up the following words. Then write the guide words found at the top of the page where you found each word. If a word ends in –s, -ed, or –ing, you have to look up the root word to find the meaning.

1. violet _____   _____

2. calling _____   _____

3. afraid _____   _____

4. wrapped _____   _____

5. fleecy _____   _____

6. overhead _____   _____

7. reeds _____   _____

8. sighing _____   _____

9. trickles _____   _____

10. hood _____   _____

11. slender _____   _____

12. shivering _____   _____

BROTHER GREEN-COAT, P. 227

Preteach and review the following vocabulary: summerhouse, scrubbed, Fairyland, soot, puzzled, trousers, crossly, language, intends, burst, tadpoles, snug, floating, whitish, jelly, and hatched.

Answer the following comprehension questions on paper.

1. Why did Betty wish that there were elves and fairies? Betty wished that there were elves and fairies so that they could enjoy the day, after a long winter.

2. Read aloud the conversation between Aunt Molly and Betty, pages 228, 229 (two pupils).

3. Tell how Aunt Molly's little friend looked each time she saw him. Aunt Molly's friend was very, very small and black as soot. He had a big head and a long tail, but no arms or legs. Then his tail got longer, and he had two legs. The next time they met, he was even bigger and had arms and legs, but no tail. The last time she saw him, he was more than a hundred times as big as at first, and he was green and white.

4. What was the name of her little friend? Her little friend's name is Brother Green-Coat.

5. What is Brother Green-Coat's name before he puts on his velvet suit? Brother Green-Coat is a tadpole before he puts on his velvet suit.

6. Where does Brother Green-Coat live in winter? Brother Green-Coat lives deep in the mud at the bottom of the pool in the winter.

7. What did Betty learn from Aunt Molly's little friend? Betty learned the different stages a frog goes through from egg to adult and where they live in the winter.

8. Read aloud the conversation on pages 231, 232 (two pupils).

9. In the picture on page 232, point to the frog's eggs; the tadpoles.

Draw a diagram of the stages of a frog's life on the worksheet.

For an extension, learn about the stages of another amphibian.

Answers: Stage 1—eggs (clear, whitish jelly, full of little black dots) Stage 2—tadpole (black, big head, long tail) Stage 3—longer tail, two legs Stage 4—no tail, arms and legs Stage 5—frog (100 times bigger, green and white)

BROTHER GREEN-COAT, p. 227

Illustrate and include a description of the different stages that a frog goes through from egg to adult.

Stage 3

[ ]

_____

_____

Stage 2

[ ]

Stage 4

[ ]

_____

_____

_____

_____

Stage 1

[ ]

Stage 5

[ ]

_____

_____

_____

_____

THE SCARECROW, p. 233

Preteach and review the following vocabulary: scarecrow, clustered, brim, bristling, fasten, tattered, blossoms, sea foam, aslant, keen, prospects, blight, comical, budge, mellow, perked, utmost, half-concealed, ease, ruby, thriving, brisk, convenient, and risk.

There are no comprehension questions for this poem.

Use the worksheet to practice inferences.

Answers: 1. The farmer wanted to beat the robins to keep them from eating his cherries. 2. The birds were scared when they first saw the scarecrow because they thought it was a real person who was going to hurt them. 3. The birds wanted to be close to the tree because they wanted to eat the ripe cherries. 4. "They ran no risk" was a way of saying the birds weren't going to get caught. They were no longer scared of the scarecrow because they built their nest in his pocket.

THE SCARECROW, p. 233

Answer the following inference questions. Remember to use clues from
the poem to prove your answers.

1. Why did the farmer want to beat the robins?

_____

_____

2. Why were the birds scared when they first saw the scarecrow?

_____

_____

3. Why did the birds want to be close to the tree?

_____

_____

4. At the end, the poem says, "They ran no risk!" What did the poet
    mean by this?

_____

_____

WHAT KEPT THE CHIMNEY WAITING?, p. 235

Preteach and review the following vocabulary: chimney, mortar, bricklayer, Frank, Walter, hodcarriers, harnessing, jolty, orchard, disappointment, plainly, crippled, brows, attic, tiptoed, thistledown, speckly, and freckly.

Answer the following comprehension questions on paper.

1. Why were the boys glad when they heard that a chimney was to be built? The boys were glad when they heard that a new chimney was to be built because they could pretend to be hodcarriers.

2. What did the grandfather show the boys, that explained why the new chimney had to wait? Grandfather showed the boys the little bird sitting on a nest with four speckly, freckly eggs.

3. What is thistledown? Thistledown is the crown of a thistle plant that contains the seeds.

Read the worksheet to review the different genres covered in this book.

Answers will vary.

WHAT KEPT THE CHIMNEY WAITING?, p. 235

This is a review of the different genres covered in this book. Read over each description and give an example of a story or poem that fits the description.

1. Fiction—a piece of literature that includes imaginary characters and events

_____

2. Nonfiction—a piece of literature that includes true facts (Include historical fiction)

_____

3. Poetry—an arrangement of words expressing experiences either real or imagined

_____

4. Drama—a literary piece that tells a story that must be acted out or performed by actors

_____

5. Fantasy—a highly imaginative piece of writing

_____

6. Biography—a true story about a person written by another

_____

7. Fable—a fictional story meant to teach a moral lesson, characters usually include talking animals

_____

8. Fairy Tale—stories about giants, fairies, and magical things

_____

NEST EGGS, p. 238

Preteach and review the following vocabulary: flutter, quarrel, arbor-like, laurel, frail, upspringing, beeches, sensible, and plodding.

Answer the following comprehension questions on paper.

1. Where was the nest built? The nest was built in a laurel.

2. What can the little birds do that the children, though older, cannot do? The birds can fly in the sky, which the children cannot do.

3. Who wrote this poem? What other poems by the same author have you read in this book? Robert Louis Stevenson wrote this poem. The other poems he has written in this book are "Farewell to the Farm" and "A Good Play."

4. Recite from memory any poem by Stevenson that you know.

5. Explain: "in the fork"; "frail eggs"; "tops of the beeches." "In the fork" means where two branches meet at the trunk. "Frail eggs" mean the eggs are very fragile. "Top of the beeches" means in the top of beech trees.

Use the worksheet to practice following step-by-step directions.

Answers: Check for following directions at every step.

NEST EGGS, p. 238

Following directions are very important. They can help keep us safe, help us get to where we want to go, and help us do fun activities. Follow the step-by-step directions to do a fun activity yourself.

1. Gather these materials: pinecone, piece of string, spoon, peanut butter, and birdseed.

2. Find a large pinecone.

3. Tie a string to the top of it.

4. Spread peanut butter all over the pinecone with a spoon.

5. Roll the pinecone in birdseed.

6. Hang your finished pinecone in a nearby tree.

7. Enjoy birdwatching!

ROBIN REDBREAST, p. 239

Preteach and review the following vocabulary: Redbreast, ruddy, breast-knot, hosts, leathery, russet, and pinching.

There are no comprehension questions for this poem.

Use the provided worksheet to learn more about root words, prefixes, and suffixes.

Answers: 1. nearly 2. smiling 3. faintly 4. sweetly 5. falling
6. leathery 7. pinching

ROBIN REDBREAST, p. 239

A root is a word or word base from which other words are made. By adding a prefix to the beginning of a root word, or a suffix to the end, you are creating new words. Sometimes an –ed or –ing is added to the end of a root word. Use the following root words to create new words by adding a prefix or suffix to the word. For example: sad can be changed to sadly. All of these words came from this poem.

1. near _____

2. smile _____

3. faint _____

4. sweet _____

5. fall _____

6. leather _____

7. pinch _____

THE SHELL, P. 240

Preteach and review the following vocabulary: shore and rushing.

There are no comprehension questions for this poem.

Practice answering the five Ws on the activity sheet provided.

Answers: 1. This poem is being told by a girl. 2. The girl has a shell. 3. This happened in the past. 4. This event takes place at the beach. 5. The girl is curious about the sounds of the shell.

THE SHELL, p. 240

A good way to truly understand what you have read is to answer the five
  Ws about it. The five Ws are: who, what, when, where, and why.
  Answer each of these Ws based on this poem.

1. Who?

_____

_____

2. What?

_____

_____

3. When?

_____

_____

4. Where?

_____

_____

5. Why?

_____

_____

Jack Frost and the Pitcher,

p. 242

Preteach and review the following vocabulary: creaked, Katrina, pitcher, crib, Jamie, icy, careless, spare, coals, frost-flakes, pity, noiselessly, washstand, groaned, repeating, several, and rattling.

Answer the following comprehension questions on paper.

1. Why did Jack Frost say that Katrina was careless? Jack Frost said that Katrina was careless because he knew she would never empty the pitcher.

2. Why did he not go into the sitting room? He did not go into the sitting room because a bright fire was gleaming in there.

3. What happened to the pitcher? The pitcher cracked because of the freezing water inside it.

4. What was Katrina doing while Jack Frost was busy? Katrina lay dreaming in her snug bed about Grandmother's pitcher dancing gaily on the bed and gliding far away on Jamie's new skate.

5. Use another word for *creaked, chuckled, glowing,* and *glide.* Another word for *creaked* is *squeaked,* for *chuckled* is *laughed,* for *glowing* is *shining,* and for *glide* is *move smoothly*.

6. Class readings: the conversation between Katrina and her mother, pages 242, 243 (two pupils); the last two paragraphs on page 246.

Use the provided worksheet for a lesson on adverbs.

Answers: 1. creaked 2. slipped 3. crept 4. slipped 5. freeze 6. dancing

JACK FROST AND THE PITCHER, p. 242

Adverbs are words that describe verbs. Many times, adverbs end in –ly. Listed below are some adverbs found in this story. Find them in the story and tell what verbs they describe.

1. loudly   _____

2. softly   _____

3. noiselessly _____

4. quickly   _____

5. certainly   _____

6. gaily   _____

SIGNS OF THE SEASONS, p. 247

Preteach and review the following vocabulary: signs, blades, ripe, flit, chirp, steer, and drifting.

There are no comprehension questions for this poem.

Use the provided worksheet to give supporting details about the seasons.

For an extension, write a journal entry about your favorite season and the activities you enjoy doing during that time of year.

Answers will vary.

SIGNS OF THE SEASONS, p. 247

Use the chart below to fill in the supporting details included in this poem about each of the four seasons. Include your own supporting details as well.

Spring

_____

_____

_____

_____

Summer

_____

_____

_____

_____

Autumn

_____

_____

_____

_____

Winter

_____

_____

_____

_____

MOTHER SPIDER, P. 248

Preteach and review the following vocabulary: midsummer, beetle, pounced, seesaw, grumbled, wriggled, exercise, wee, tire, weight, and worth.

Answer the following comprehension questions on paper.

1. Which of the little creatures mentioned on page 248 have you seen? The little creatures mentioned on page 248 are ants, a toad, bees, a robin, a spider, a beetle, and a grasshopper.

2. What did Mother Spider carry in her mouth this summer day? Mother Spider was holding a little white bag in her mouth.

3. What was in her white bag? There were baby spiders in the white bag.

4. What did she carry on her back at a later time, when Grasshopper Green met her? Mother Spider was carrying wee baby spiders on her back.

5. Use another word for *pounced*. Another word for *pounced* is *jumped*.

6. Read the conversation between Mother Spider and Grasshopper Green (two pupils).

Review contractions by using the provided worksheet.

Answers: 1. didn't 2. needn't 3. aren't 4. doesn't 5. don't 6. couldn't 7. shouldn't 8.-10. Answers will vary.

MOTHER SPIDER, p. 248

Remember that contractions are words that are made up of two separate words. When you write a contraction, some letters of the second word are dropped and an apostrophe is put in its place. Write the contractions for the following words.

Choose three contractions to use in a sentence.

1. did not   _____

2. need not   _____

3. are not   _____

4. does not   _____

5. do not   _____

6. could not   _____

7. should not   _____

8. _____

   _____

9. _____

   _____

10. _____

   _____

A Song of Joy, p. 251

Preteach and review the following vocabulary: willow, buds, wren, oriole, pewee, warbler, cuckoo, and clucks.

Answer the following section questions about the outdoor world. What did you learn from the last story that makes you think Aunt Molly was right when she told Betty that some of us live in Fairyland without knowing it? Which story in this part of the book did you like best?

Review homophones by using the provided worksheet.

As an extension, design a crossword puzzle by using the eight sets of homophones. Use the definitions as clues.

Answers: 1. we 2. tails 3. sale 4. fair 5. pare or pair 6. high 7. might 8. bow   Sentences will vary, but check for correct usage of each word.

A SONG OF JOY, p. 251

You have learned that homophones are words that sound alike but have different spellings and meanings. Write a homophone to go with each word given. Then use the second word in a sentence.

1. wee   _____

_____

2. tales   _____

_____

3. sail   _____

_____

4. fare   _____

_____

5. pear   _____

_____

6. hi   _____

_____

7. mite   _____

_____

8. beau   _____

_____

THE SLEEPING BEAUTY, p. 252

Preteach and review the following vocabulary: thirteen, eleven, spindle, fate, orders, maiden, tower, rusty, flax, merrily, stables, pigeons, flaming, hearth, roasting, hedge, enchanted, forgetful, slumbering, and stooped.

Answer the following comprehension questions on paper.

1. Why did the king invite only twelve of the fairies to the feast? The king invited only twelve of the fairies to the feast because they only had twelve golden plates.

2. What did the wicked fairy do? The wicked fairy said that when the princess is fifteen years old, she will prick herself with a spindle and fall dead.

3. What was the twelfth fairy's gift? The twelfth fairy said the princess wouldn't die, but would fall into deep sleep and will awake at the end of a hundred years.

4. Tell what happened to the maiden on the day she became fifteen. The maiden was left in the palace alone so she went about looking from room to room. She came to the tower of the palace and found an old woman with a spindle. The maiden pricked her finger and sank into a deep sleep.

5. Read lines that tell of this deep sleep that fell upon the whole palace. "And this sleep fell upon all in the palace. The king and queen, who had just come home, fell asleep. The horses went to sleep in the stables, the pigeons upon the roof of the palace, and the flies upon the wall. Even the fire that was flaming on the hearth became quiet, and slept. The meat stopped roasting. The cook, who was just about to scold the kitchen boy because he had forgotten something, suddenly fell asleep. At the same moment, the wind became still, and on the great trees in front of the castle not a leaf moved again."

6. What were the words of the young prince when he heard the story of the enchanted castle? The young prince said, "I will find this Sleeping Beauty and wake her!"

7. How did he wake the princess? The young prince stooped and kissed Sleeping Beauty to wake her.

Use the provided worksheet to practice sequencing.

Answers: 4, 6, 2, 7, 8, 3, 5, 9, 1

THE SLEEPING BEAUTY, p. 252

Put the following story events in the order in which they happened.

_____ The king ordered that all of the spindles in the kingdom be burned.

_____ The princess pricked her finger, and a deep sleep fell all around the castle.

_____ Angry at not being invited, the thirteenth fairy wished for the girl to prick her finger after her fifteenth birthday and die.

_____ Thorns grew all over the castle.

_____ A prince came and awoke the princess with a kiss.

_____ The twelfth fairy wished that the child wouldn't die but instead, would go into a deep sleep.

_____ On her fifteenth birthday, when the king and queen were called away from home, the girl found her way up to the palace tower.

_____ The prince married the princess, and they lived happily ever after.

_____ The king and queen finally had a child and had a party to celebrate.

CINDERELLA, OR THE LITTLE GLASS SLIPPER, p. 258

Preteach and review the following vocabulary: Cinderella, selfish, daughters, scour, length, bore, patiently, cinders, habit, satin, diamonds, obliged, godmother, sobbing, sighing, rind, wand, mousetrap, request, coachman, rattrap, lizards, footmen, slippers, midnight, greet, ballroom, murmur, admired, midst, quarter, hastened, Charlotte, lend, warning, overtake, stroke, pardon, treatment, and charring.

Answer the following comprehension questions on paper.

1. Why was the youngest of the sisters called Cinderella? The youngest of the sisters was called Cinderella because she often went into the chimney corner and sat down among the cinders after she had finished her work.

2. Tell of Cinderella's two sisters and their mother. Cinderella's two sisters and mother were proud and selfish. The mother gave Cinderella the hardest work in the house. The younger of her two sisters was not quite so rude as the other.

3. How did her fairy godmother prepare Cinderella to go to the ball? The fairy godmother prepared Cinderella for the ball by turning a pumpkin into a coach, six mice into large white horses, a rat into a coachman, and six lizards into footmen. Then she touched Cinderella with her wand and turned her rags into fine cloth and on her feet she made Cinderella a pair of glass slippers.

4. At what time was Cinderella to return home? Cinderella was to return home by midnight.

5. How was she received at the ball? Everyone at the ball thought Cinderella was beautiful and admired how gracefully she danced with the prince.

6. Why did Cinderella wish to go to the ball again on the next night? Cinderella wished to go to the ball the next night because the king's son had asked her to come.

7. What happened when the clock struck twelve? When the clock struck twelve, Cinderella ran quickly from the ballroom, and one of her glass slippers fell off. The prince could not catch her, but he picked up her glass slipper.

8. How did the prince find the owner of the little glass slipper? The prince found the owner of the little glass slipper by sending out

a messenger to try the slipper on every lady.

9. Find lines which show that Cinderella forgave her sisters for their unkind treatment of her. "Cinderella lifted them up and put her arms around them. With all her heart, she forgave them and begged them to love her always."

10. Tell the story of Cinderella, following this outline: (a) Cinderella's selfish sisters; (b) The fairy godmother; (c) Cinderella at the ball; (d) The glass slipper.

For an extension, find another version of the Cinderella story. Read and make comparisons to this version. You may even want to put your comparisons on a chart.

Use the following worksheet to practice story elements.

Answers: These may vary.

1. Cinderella, or The Little Glass Slipper 2. Charles Perrault 3. Cinderella's home, Prince's castle 4. Cinderella, two sisters, prince, godmother 5. Cinderella wants to go to the ball, slipper's owner needs to be found 6. Godmother makes it possible for Cinderella to go to the ball, slipper is tried on Cinderella

Cinderella, or the Little Glass Slipper, p. 258

Story elements are the parts of the story that give it structure. Sometimes there are several main characters, problems, and solutions. Give the story elements with each of the listed parts.

1. **Titles**

   _____

   _____

2. **Author**

   _____

   _____

3. **Setting**

   _____

   _____

4. **Main Characters**

   _____

   _____

5. **Problems**

   _____

   _____

6. **Solutions**

   _____

   _____

FAIRYLAND, p. 270

Preteach and review the following vocabulary: garlands, nurse, dimpled, and grand.

There are no comprehension questions for this poem.

Use the provided worksheet to review compound words and create your own imaginary place.

Answers: afternoon, sometimes, westward, fairyland Sentences will vary.

FAIRYLAND, p. 270

Remember that compound words are made from two or more words. See if you can find the four compound words in this poem. Write each in a sentence.

1. _____

_____

2. _____

_____

3. _____

_____

4. _____

_____

Write about your own "fairyland." Use descriptive words and feeling to tell about it. Illustrate your enchanted place.

_____

_____

_____

_____

_____

_____

_____

_____

HANS AND THE FOUR GREAT GIANTS, p. 271

Preteach and review the following vocabulary: Hans, bundle, blacksmith, broad, gatekeeper, replied, matter, necklace, growled, noonday, hearty, exclaimed, seeking, earache, and faithfully.

Answer the following comprehension questions on paper.

1. What kind of boy was Hans? Hans was a happy little fellow who was always busy doing something for somebody.

2. Why did he go out to find work? Hans went out into the world because he needed to learn how to take care of himself.

3. Why did Hans go in search of the enchanted pearls? Hans went in search of the enchanted pearls so that he could serve the beautiful princess.

4. Tell of the trip to the North Sea. On the trip to the North Sea, Hans met four great giants who agreed to come along and help him get the pearls and take them to the king.

5. How did Hans win the princess? Hans won the princess by getting the enchanted pearls and serving her so faithfully that she fell in love with him.

6. Do you think he deserved his good fortune? Yes, Hans deserved his good fortune because he was a good person.

7. Read lines which show that Hans was grateful. "You may be sure that Hans took good care of his old father and mother. He also asked his four friends, the giants, to come and live in his kingdom."

8. Tell the story, following this outline: (a) Hans goes out into the world; (b) The enchanted pearls; (c) Hans wins the princess.

9. Class reading: the conversation between Hans and the four giants, pages 273, 274, 275, 276, 277 (five pupils); Hans wins the princess, pages 278, 279.

Use the provided worksheet to explore character analysis.

Answers: Answers will vary, but here is a sample: Hans—happy, tall, strong, helpful; Giant 1—large, strong, fast walker; Giant 2—strong eyes; Giant 3—long arms; Giant 4—great hearing, good-natured; Gatekeeper—helpful; King—challenger, pleased; Princess—beautiful, loved Hans, became queen

HANS AND THE FOUR GREAT GIANTS, p. 271

Character analysis is a way looking at a person in many ways, such as
how they look, what they do, and how they act. Use notes, not
complete sentences, to describe everything you can about each of
the following characters.

Hans—

_____

Giant 1—

_____

Giant 2—

_____

Giant 3—

_____

Giant 4—

_____

Gatekeeper—

_____

King—

_____

Princess—

_____

THE UGLY DUCKLING, p. 280

Preteach and review the following vocabulary: ugly, duckling, burdock, cheated, tumbled, yonder, Spanish, handsome, bitten, teased, puffed, gobbles, spurs, worse, cruelly, marsh, jaws, clever, sensible, plunge, sunset, slender, splendid, suffered, bore, thicket, curved, image, and swan.

Have your child answer the following comprehension questions on paper.

1. How did the mother duck find out that the ugly little one was not a turkey? Mother Duck found out that the ugly little one was not a turkey when she could see how well it could swim.

2. Why was the duckling not liked in the farmyard or in the hut? The duckling was not liked in the farmyard or in the hut because he was so large and ugly.

3. Why did the duckling wish to be beautiful? The duckling wished to be beautiful so the other animals would like him.

4. Do you think the duckling would have been called "ugly" if he had always lived with the swans? No, the duckling would not have been called ugly if he had always lived with the swans because that is the way all young swans look.

5. Read lines that tell how happy the duckling was when he was called beautiful. "The young swan hid his head under his wing, for he was so happy that he did not know what to do. He was almost too happy, but he was not proud."

6. Use another word for *handsome, plunge, reeds, slender,* and *image.* Another word for *handsome* is *beautiful,* for *plunge* is *dip,* for *reeds* is *tall grasses,* for *slender* is *narrow,* and for *image* is *reflection.*

7. Tell the story, following this outline: (a) The great egg; (b) In the farmyard; (c) In the hut; (d) The beautiful swan.

8. Class readings: the conversation between the mother duck and the friendly duck, page 281; the conversation of the mother duck and the Spanish duck, page 284; the conversation in the hut, pages 286, 287, 288, 289 (four pupils).

Use the provided worksheet to practice main ideas.

Answers: The Great Egg—The duck had a very large egg in her

nest that she was determined to hatch. In the Farmyard—Everyone made fun of the new hatchling because he was so funny looking. In the Hut—The cat and the hen wanted the duckling to act just like them. The Beautiful Swan—The ugly duckling was actually a beautiful swan.

THE UGLY DUCKLING, p. 280

For each of the following chapters, write the main idea. Include an illustration that goes with what you wrote.

The Great Egg—

In the Farmyard—

In the Hut—

The Beautiful Swan—

VACATION TIME, p. 294

There are no new vocabulary words.

Answer the following section questions. Which story in this group did you like best? Which story did you like best in the entire book? Which poem in this book did you like best?

Recite from memory any lines of poetry you have memorized from this book.

Use the following worksheet to practice outlining.

Answers will vary.

VACATION TIME, p. 294

Outlining is an organized way of putting your thoughts down. An outline is a wonderful way to prepare your notes to be used in a piece of writing. Use the following outline to give your ideas about summer vacation. List two things you want to do in each of the three months. Fill these in where you see the letters A and B.

Vacation

I.   June

  A._____

  B._____

II. July

  A._____

  B._____

III. August

  A._____

  B._____

Now use this outline to write an essay about your summer vacation.

_____

_____

_____

_____

_____

_____

WORD LIST

a as in m<u>a</u>t   ə as in b<u>a</u>nana   ä as in f<u>a</u>ther   ∅ as in s<u>i</u>de
e as in b<u>e</u>d   ər as in fur<u>ther</u>   aù as in l<u>ou</u>d   ŋ as in si<u>ng</u>
i as in t<u>i</u>p   ā as in d<u>a</u>y   ē as in n<u>ee</u>d   ō as in sn<u>o</u>w
ȯ as in s<u>a</u>w   ȯi as in c<u>oi</u>n   ü as in rule   ủ as in p<u>u</u>ll
ᵊ as in eat<u>e</u>n   <u>th</u> as in hea<u>th</u>er

A

act ('akt) part

ac tive ('ak-tiv) quick; nimble

ad ven ture (ad-ven-'ture) a remarkable happening

Aeolus ('ē-ə-ləs)

aid ('ād) help

Ai ken Drum ('ā-kən)

Aire dales ('ar-dəlz) a kind of dog

air y ('ar-ē) breezy

a light (ə-'l∅t) come to rest

al li ga tor ('a-lə-gā-tər) a large animal that lives in the water

all to her mind of just the kind she liked

al mond ('ä-mənd) a nut

al tered ('ȯl-tərd) changed

am bu lance ('am-byə-ləns) long covered car in which wounded men are carried

a mus ing (a-'myü-ziŋ) funny

anx ious ly ('aŋk-shəs-lē) eagerly

ar bor-like ('är-bər-l∅k) like a shelter made of vines or trees

ar bu tus (är-'byü-təs) an early spring flower

ar gue ('är-gyü) try to make her change her mind

ar mor ('är-mər) metal covering worn to protect the body in battle

a slant (ə-'slant) on one side

at any rate well; at least

at tend (ə-'tend) heed; care for

au tumn ('ȯ-təm) fall

awk ward ('ȯ-kwerd) clumsy

B

bade ('bād) ordered; told

ball ('bȯl) fine party with dancing

band ('band) several together

banks ('baŋks) sides of earth or rock
bare ('bar) leafless; without grass
beak ('bēk) bill
beat ('bēt) get ahead of
be cause (bi-'kȯz)
beech ('bēch) a kind of tree
be lo ved (be-'lə-vəd) dear; loved
Beth le hem ('beth-lə-hem)
bil lows ('bi-lōz) great waves
bit ter ly ('bi-tər-li) painfully; hard
blast ('blast) long note
bleat ('blēt) noise made by sheep
Bled nock ('bled-näk)
bloom ('blüm) blossom
boast ('bōst) brag
bold ly ('bōld-lē) as if he were not afraid
bore ('bōr) endured; lived; held
boughs ('baủs) branches
bowed ('baud) bend
brains ('brānz) wise thoughts
breast knot ('brest-nät) feathers on the breast
brisk ('brisk) quick; lively
bris tling ('bris-liŋ) angry; threatening
bronze ('bränz) a reddish metal
budge ('bəj) move
bur dock ('bər-däk) a common weed
burst ('berst) come suddenly
busi ness ('biz-nəs) what one has to do
butt ('bət) strike with the head

C

Ca naan ('kā-nən)
cap ture ('kap-chər) take by force
car a van ('kar-ə-van) a number of people traveling together
car ol ('kar-əl) song of praise; Christmas hymn; sing
cer tain ly ('sər-tən-lē) surely
Chank ly Bore ('chank-lē; 'bōr)
charge ('chärj) a duty or task given one to do
char i ot ('char-ē-ət) a kind of carriage
charm ing ('chär-miŋ) pleasing; beautiful; delightful
cheat ed ('chē-təd) fooled
chil ly ('chi-lē) cold

chink ('chiŋk) crack

chip ('chip) break open

chis el ('chi-zəl) long, sharp tool

chris ten ing ('kris-niŋ) church service where a baby is named

chuck le ('chə-kəl) laugh to oneself

churn ('chərn) tub or jar for making butter; stir; beat

cin ders ('sin-dərz) ashes

claimed ('klāmd) said he had a right to

clasped ('klaspt) took hold of and held firmly

clat ter ('kla-tər) rattling noise

clev er ('kle-vər) sharp; cunning

cling ('kliŋ) hold fast

cloak ('klōk) loose coat

clump ('kləmp) group of bushes or trees

clum sy ('kləm-zē) awkward

clus ter ('kləs-tər) bunch

coach and pair ('kōch; 'pār) fine carriage drawn by two horses

coach man ('kōch-man) driver

cock ('käk) rooster

col lie ('kä-lē) large, shepherd dog

com fort ('kəm-fərt) cheer

com i cal ('kä-mi-kəl) laughable

com mand (kə-'mand) order; control; rule

com plain (kəm-'plān) find fault; grumble

con cealed (kən-'sēld) hidden

con fused (kən-'fyüz) bothered so they could not think clearly

con stant ('kän-stənt) going on all the time

con tent ed (kən-'ten-təd) satisfied

con ven ient (kən-'vēn-yənt) easy; handy

con vent ('kän-vənt) home of monks or nuns

Co sette (kō-'zet)

co vert ('kō-vərt) shelter; hiding place

crag gy ('kra-gē) covered with rough, broken rocks

creaked ('krēkt) squeaked

cre a tion (krē-'ā-shən) world, sun, moon, and stars

crea ture ('krē-chər) any live thing

crisp ('krisp) thin and dry; easily broken

croak ing ('krō-kiŋ) a frog's cry

crushed ('krəsht) mashed

cuckoo ('kü-kü) a brown bird

curb ('kərb) edge of the sidewalk next to the street

cur i ous flight ('kyur-ē-əs) strange way of flying

curt sied ('kərt-sēd) bowed

D

dain ty ('dān-tē) delicate; pleasant; something good to eat

daren't ('dar-ənt) do not dare

dar ing ('dar-iŋ) bold

dawn ('don) daybreak

de clined (di-'klØnd) refused

deed ('dēd) act

de lay (di-'lā) put off; waste time; make lose time

de li cious (de-'li-shəs) delightful; pleasing to the taste

de light (di-'lØt) happiness; joy

de light ful (di-'lØt-fəl) very pleasant

dell ('del) small valley

den ('den) home of a wild animal

dew y ('dü-ē) wet with dew

Di e go (dē-'ā-gō)

dim pled ('dim-pəld) having little hollows like dimples

dis ap peared (di-sə-'pird) went out of sight

dis cour aged (dis-'ker-ijd) be discouraged, lose heart; give up

down ('daùn) soft, fluffy feathers

drag on ('dra-gən) an imagined creature of great fierceness

droop ('drüp) bend over

duck ling ('dek-liŋ) little duck

dumb ('dəm) quiet

dunce ('dəns) stupid person

dusk ('dəsk) dim light just before dark

dwarf ('dwörf) a tiny person

E

ea ger ('ē-gər) ready to do or go

ear nest ('ər-nəst) thoughtful; serious

ef fect (i-'fekt) result

ef fort ('e-fərt) attempt

E gypt ('i-jipt)

elf ('elf) a fairy

en chant ed (in-'chan-təd) magic

en rolled (in-'rōld) put on the list

ere ('er) before

ev er more (e-vər-'mōr) always; forever

evil ('ē-vəl) wrongdoing; wrong

ex press (ik-'spres) tell

ex treme ly (ik-'strēm-lē) very

F

faint ('fānt) not bright or plain; weak

fair ('far) pretty; good-looking; sweet

faith ful ('fāth-fəl) true; steady

fam ine ('fa-mən) need of food

fared ('fard) got along

fare well (far-'wel) good-bye

fash ioned ('fa-shənd) made

fate ('fāt) fortune; unhappy end

fa vor ite ('fā-və-rət) liked more than another

fierce ('firs) furious; violent

fi er y ('f∅-ə-rē) looking like fire

firm ('fərm) without moving at all

firmly ('fərm-lē) tightly

flat ter ('fla-tər) please with praise which is not true

flax ('flaks) the fiber of the plant from which linen is made

fled ('fled) ran away

fleece ('flēs) sheep's wool

flee cy ('flē-sē) like the wool of a sheep

flight ('fl∅t) flying; way of flying

flit ('flit) fly quickly

flung ('flung) threw quickly

flut ter ('flə-tər) move about excitedly; wave back and forth; fly

fod der-corn ('fä-dər) dry cornstalks

folk ('fōk) people

foot men ('füt-mən) men servants

for est ('fȯr-əst) thick woods

fork ('fȯrk) place where a large branch parts into two smaller ones

form ing ('fȯr-miŋ) getting ready to march

for tune ('fȯr-chən) success; luck

for ward ('fȯr-wərd) ahead

fox glove ('fäks-gləv) a kind of flower growing along a high stalk

frail ('frā-əl) easily broken; weak

Fran çois (fran-'swä)

fret ful ('fret-fəl) likely to cry

fri ar ('fr∅-ər) a kind of monk

frock ('fräk) dress

front ('frənt) battle line where the fighting goes on

fros ty ('frȯ-stē) covered with frost

fur nish ings ('fer-nish-iŋz) furniture and decorations

fur rows (ˈfər-ōs) open spaces between the rows

G

gar den er (ˈgär-dən-ər) one who works in a garden

gar land (ˈgär-lənd) wreath

gar ment (ˈgär-mənt) dress; clothing

gath er (ˈga-thər) draw close

gay (ˈgā) happy; bright; joyful

glade (ˈglād) open place in a wood

glance (ˈglans) quick look

gleam (ˈglēm) flash; shine

glen (ˈglen) narrow valley

glide (ˈglØd) move smoothly along

glimpse (ˈglimps) a quick sight

glit ter ing (ˈgli-tə-riŋ) shining

globe (ˈglōb) ball; sphere

glow (ˈglō) brightness; shine

god moth er (ˈgäd-mə-thər) a woman who promises when a child is chris-
tened to help it

good-na tured ly (gu̇d-ˈnā-chərd-lē) kindly

good-temp ered (gu̇d-ˈtəm-pərd) pleasant; kind

grace ful ly (ˈgrās-fə-lē) with light pretty movements

grant (ˈgrant) allow; permit

grasped (ˈgraspt) took hold of

Greek (ˈgrēk) living in Greece

greet (ˈgrēt) welcome

grief (ˈgrēf) sorrow; distress

grim (ˈgrim) fierce; stern

gros beak (ˈgrōs-bēk) a bird with a large thick bill

ground (ˈgrau̇nd) pressed hard

guard (ˈgärd) protect from danger; defend

H

hand ker chief (ˈhaŋ-kər-chəf)

hand some (ˈhan-səm) good-looking; **handsome is as handsome does**, how
you act matters more than how you look

hare (ˈhar) rabbit

haste (ˈhāst) hurry

has ten (ˈhā-sən) hurry

hearth (ˈhärth) fireplace

heart y (ˈhär-tē) great; cheerful

hedge (ˈhej) fence of bushes

hedge hog (ˈhej-hȯg) a small animal covered with prickles

heed ('hēd) pay attention to

hel met ('hel-mət) a covering for the head in battle

hel ter skel ter ('hel-tər; 'skel-tər) in hurry and disorder

hob gob lin ('häb-gäb-lən) mischievous elf or goblin; brownie

home spun (hōm-'spən) woven at home; coarse; plain

hon or ('ä-nər) respect; sign of favor

hor ri ble ('hȯr-ə-bəl) shocking; terrible

hos pi tal ('häs-pi-təl) a place in which sick people are cared for

host ('hōst) a great number

huge ('hyüj) very large; great

hurled ('hər-əld) thrown hard

hut ('hət) poor, small house

I

ill-tem pered (il-'tem-pərd) cross

im age ('i-mij) picture

inn ('in) hotel

in stant ly ('in-stənt-lē) that very minute

in sult ('in-səlt) be very rude to

in tend ed (in-'ten-dəd) planned

in ter rupt (in-tə-'rəpt) talk when some one else is talking

Is ra el ('iz-rē-əl) the Hebrews; the Jewish people

J

jack daw ('jak-dȯ) a black bird

Jacques ('zhak)

Ja pan (jə-'pan) the group of islands east of Asia

Jeanne ('zhan)

jin gling ('jiŋ-gliŋ) rattling

jol li est ('jä-lē-əst) gayest

jolt ('jōlt) jerk

jos tle ('jä-səl) push and crowd

jour ney ('jer-nē) trip

joy ful ly ('jȯi-fə-lē) happily; very gladly

K

Kat ri na (ka-'trē-na)

keep er ('kē-per) one who guards or takes care of

ker nel ('kər-nəl) inside part which we eat

knight ('nØt) man who had promised to help any who were in trouble

L

lan guage ('lan-gwij) speech

lau rel ('lȯr-əl) an evergreen tree or shrub

lawn ('lȯn) ground covered with grass

leaped (ˈlēpt) jumped

leath er y (ˈle-thə-rē) dry, tough

ledge (ˈlej) little outside shelf

leg end (ˈle-jənd) old story

lin ger (ˈliŋ-gər) stay or wait long; go slowly

liz ard (ˈli-zərd) a little creeping animal

loi ter (ˈlòi-tər) move slowly; stop to play

lol li pop (ˈlä-li-päp) a kind of candy

long ing (ˈloŋ-iŋ) wishing very much

look out (ˈlùk-aùt) watch; one who watches

lot (ˈlät) fortune; fate

lowed (ˈlōd) mooed softly

M

mac a roon (ˈmak-ə-rün) a small cake

mal let (ˈma-lət) wooden hammer

man aged (ˈma-nijd) done

Man i tou (ˈma-nə-tù) the Indian name for God

marsh (ˈmärsh) soft wet land partly covered with water

marsh mar i gold (ˈmärsh; ˈmar-ə-gōld) a yellow flower that grows in wet
   places

mate (ˈmāt) wife; companion

mea dow (ˈme-dō) grassy field

meet ing house (ˈmēt-iŋ ˈhaùs) church

mel low (ˈme-lō) ripe

mer chant (ˈmər-chənt) man who buys and sells

mer ry (ˈmer-ē) jolly

might y (ˈmᴓt-ē) powerful

mild (ˈmᴓld) gentle; kind

mill (ˈmil) place where grain is ground

mil let (ˈmi-lət) a kind of grass

mind (ˈmᴓnd) tend; object to

mis chief (ˈmis-chəf) harm

mi ser (ˈmᴓ-zər) one who has riches but lives poorly

moc ca sin (ˈmä-kə-sən) loose shoe made of one piece of leather

mon ster (ˈmän-stər) strange or horrible animal

mor tar (ˈmòr-tər) lime mixed with sand and water

moss es (ˈmò-səz) tiny, soft green plants

moun ting (ˈmäun-tiŋ) climbing; getting upon

mourn (ˈmōrn) be sorry; grieve

mur mur (ˈmər-mər) make a low sound

muse (ˈmyüz) think about

N

Nan nette (na-'net)

na tal ('nā-təl) of birth

nay ('nā) no

ne'er ('nar) never

neigh bor ('nā-bər) one who lives near another

neighed ('nād) whinnied

nip ('nip) bite off

no ble ('nō-bəl) splendid; very fine

nook ('nuk) little spot

O

o be di ent (ō-'bē-dē-ənt) doing what one is told to do

o bliged (ō-'blijd) forced; bound

o'er ('ōr) over; past

old en ('ōl-dən) very old; long ago

o ri ole ('ōr-ē-ōl) a small black and orange-colored bird

o ver come (ō-vər-'kəm) gain victory over; got over

o ver flowed (ō-vər-'flōd) rose above

o ver take (ō-vər-'tāk) catch up with

ox hide ('äks-hØd) leather made from the skin of an ox

P

page ('pāj) boy who waited upon the people in the palace

Pa los ('pa-lōs)

pa poose (pa-'püs) Indian baby

par cel ('pär-səl) bundle; package

pas ture ('pas-chər) grassy place

patch ('pach) garden; spot

pa tient ly ('pā-shənt-lē) without complaint

pat ty ('pa-tē) small pie

Pe bo an ('pē-bō-an)

peer ('pir) look curiously

Pe rez ('per-əs)

per fect ly ('pər-fikt-lē) entirely; exactly

perk ('pərk) straighten up; show off

pet al ('pe-tᵊl) one of the small leaves which make up a flower

pe wee ('pē-wē) a little greenish gray bird

pierce ('pirs) make a way through

plain ('plān) clear; simple; not rich; a level country

plan ta tion (plan-'tā-shən) farm

plead ('plēd) ask earnestly; beg; offer as excuse

plen ti ful ('plen-ti-fəl) full; rich; having enough

plod ('pläd) walk heavily and slowly
plunge ('plənj) dive into; fall; jump
point ('pȯint) little thing
pol ish ('pä-lesh) rub until they shine; make smooth or shiny
po si tion (pə-'zi-shən) place
pounce ('paůns) jump quickly
pranc ing ('pran-siŋ) springing
pray ('prā) beg; please
prec ious ('pre-shəs) of great value
pre fer ('pri-fər) like better; rather have
pre pare (pri-'par) make ready
pres ent ly ('pre-zᵊnt-lē) soon; after a while
pressed ('prest) ironed flat
prompt ('prämpt) ready quick; on time
prop er ('prä-pər) own; which belongs to it
psalm ('säm) a sacred song or poem
pump kin ('pəmp-kəm)
puz zled ('pə-zəld) confused

R

rage ('rāj) great anger
rays ('rāz) beams of light
rear ing ('rir-iŋ) jumping around
re count ed (rē-'kaůn-təd) told again and again
red poll ('red-pōl) a small bird with a red head
reed ('rēd) tall grass growing in water
re gain (ri-'gān) get back
re joiced (ri-'jȯist) was glad
re quest (ri-'kwest) thing asked
res cued ('res-kyüd) freed; helped out of trouble
re ward (re-'wərd) pay for doing something
rich ('rich) fancy; costly; wealthy
rind ('rɵnd) outer hard skin
ring-bo ree ('riŋ-bō-rē)
rip en ing ('rɵ-pə-niŋ) becoming ripe
robe ('rōb) flowing dress; decorations
rooks ('růks) large black birds
rough ('rəf) not well drawn
roy al ('rȯi-əl) such as a king might have
rud dy ('rə-dē) red
Ru pert ('rü-pərt)
rush y ('rə-shē) full of rushes—plants growing in wet places

rus set ('rə-sət) brown because dried up

rut ('rət) track worn by wheels

S

sad dles ('sa-dᵊlz) blankets with pockets

sat is fied ('sa-təs-fᴓd) contented; happy

sau cy ('sȯ-sē) rude in a good-natured way

scant y ('skan-tē) very small; not enough

scorch ing ('skȯr-chiŋ) burning

scorn ('skȯrn) lack of respect

scram ble ('skram-bəl) climb on his hands and knees

scuf fling ('skə-fə-liŋ) good-natured rough play

sea foam ('sē; 'fōm) white mass of tiny bubbles on the shore

search ('sərch) hunt; look for

Seeg wun ('sēg-wən)

seize ('sēz) grab; take by force

sen ti nel ('sent-ᵊn-əl) soldier who watches while others sleep

serve ('sərv) work for; wait upon; do things for others; treat

sheaves ('shēvs) bundles

shep herd ('she-pərd) one who tends sheep

shield ('shēld) a frame of metal or wood carried on the arm in battle to keep off blows

shiv er ed ('shi-vərd) trembled

shrill ('shril) high and sharp

shud der ('shə-dər) tremble; shiver; trembling

shy ('shᴓ) timid

sieve ('siv) a sifter

si lence ('sᴓ-ləns) quiet

si lent ly ('sᴓ-lənt-lē) quietly

sim ple ton ('sim-pəl-tən) silly person

sis kin ('sis-kən) small bird

slen der ('slen-dər) long and slim

slum ber ('sləm-bər) sleep

sly ('slᴓ) tricky; cunning

snug ('snəg) cozy; comfortable

snug gle ('snə-gəl) cuddle

sound ('saůnd) hard

spare ('spar) more than enough; give up; **spare room** bedroom kept for company

spark led ('spär-kəld) shone; twinkled

speech less ('spēch-ləs) unable to speak

spell ('spel) magic charm

spin dle ('spin-dᵊl) a round pointed stick with a notch to hold the yarn while spinning

spite ('spᴓt) ill will; meanness

splen did ('splen-dəd) very fine; grand; glorious

spray ('sprā) little branch

sprin kled ('spriŋ-kəld) scattered

squint ('skwint) partly close his eyes in trying to see better

squirm ('skərm) twist about; wriggle

stack ('stak) pile up

staff ('staf) long stick

stared ('stard) looked suprised

steals ('stēlz) walks carefully

steer ('stir) turn their flight

Stef an ('ste-fən)

store house ('stōr-haủs) building where things are put away

stream ('strēm) river or creek; shine straight in

stretch er bear ers ('stre-chər; 'bar-ərz) men who carry wounded on stretchers

strug gle ('strə-gəl) work hard; fight

stu dy ('stə-dē) room where one studies

stunned ('stənd) senseless; unable to move

stu pid ('stü-pəd) dull; foolish

suc cess (sək-'ses) good results

su et ('sü-ət) beef fat

swamp ('swämp) wet, low ground

swan ('swän) large, white bird

swarmed ('swȯrmd) seemed to be many and all moving in different ways

sway ing ('swā-iŋ) moving gently

swift ('swift) very quick; fast

T

task ('task) work; lesson

tat tered ('ta-tərd) ragged

Ta wa ra (ta-'wa-ra)

tend ed ('ten-dəd) took care of

ten der ly ('ten-dər-lē) gently; lovingly

ter ri er ('ter-ē-ər) a small dog

test ('test) examine; try

this tle down ('thi-səl-daủn) the soft, feathery, ripe thistle

throne room ('thrōn-rüm) room where the king meets his visitors

ti dings ('tᴓ-diŋz) news

ti dy ('tᴓ-dē) neat; put in order

tilt ('tilt) seesaw

Tor ri ble Zone ('tȯr-ə-bəl; 'zōn)

to ward ('tō-ərd) in the direction of

trav el er ('tra-və-lər) person going from one place to another

treas ure ('tre-zhər) riches; things of great value

treat ('trēt) something which gives great pleasure; deal with

trem bling ('trem-bə-liŋ) shaking

trench es ('tren-chəz) long, deep ditches in which men fought

troop ('trüp) move in crowds; large number

trou bled ('trə-bəld) worried

tru ant ('trü-ənt) one who stays away from school when one should go

twin kle ('twiŋ-kəl) gleam; look

U

U lys ses (yu̇-'li-sēz)

un self ish ness (ən-'sel-fish-nəs) care and thought for others

up ris ing (əp-'r∅-ziŋ) flying up

up roar ('əp-rōr) great noise

ut most ('ət-mōst) greatest

V

vale ('vāl) little valley

val ley ('va-lē) low ground between hills

veil ('vāl) very thin scarf

vic to ry ('vik-tə-rē) winning of a battle; success in a fight

voy age ('vȯi-ij) trip on the sea

W

wa ges ('wā-jəz) pay for work

wal let ('wä-lət) bag

wand ('wänd) fairy's magic stick

wan der ('wän-dər) walk about

warb ler ('wȯr-blər) a small song bird

war rior ('wȯr-ē-ər) soldier

weep ('wēp) cry

whip poor will ('hwi-pər-wil) a bird named from its call

whirl ('hwərl) turn round quickly; drive

wig wam ('wig-wäm) Indian hut or tent

will ful ('wil-fəl) fond of his own way

won der ('wən-dər) surprise

wood land land covered with trees

wood land ('wu̇d-lənd) land covered with trees

Y

yon ('yän) that

Your Majesty ('yōr; 'ma-jə-stē) a polite name for the king

Books Available from
Lost Classics Book Company
American History

Stories of Great Americans for Little Americans .... Edward Eggleston
A First Book in American History .... Edward Eggleston
A History of the United States and Its People.................................. Edward Eggleston

Biography

The Life of Kit Carson.. Edward Ellis

English Grammar

Primary Language Lessons.. Emma Serl
Intermediate Language Lessons... Emma Serl
(Teacher's Guides available for each of these texts)

Elson Readers Series

Complete Set .... William Elson, Lura Runkel, Christine Keck
The Elson Readers: Primer.. William Elson, Lura Runkel
The Elson Readers: Book One .... William Elson, Lura Runkel
The Elson Readers: Book Two .... William Elson, Lura Runkel
The Elson Readers: Book Three ....William Elson
The Elson Readers: Book Four ....William Elson
The Elson Readers: Book Five .... William Elson, Christine Keck
The Elson Readers: Book Six .... William Elson, Christine Keck
The Elson Readers: Book Seven... William Elson, Christine Keck
The Elson Readers: Book Eight.. William Elson, Christine Keck
(Teacher's Guides available for each reader in this series)

Historical Fiction

With Lee in Virginia .... G. A. Henty
A Tale of the Western Plains... G. A. Henty
The Young Carthaginian... G. A. Henty
In the Heart of the Rockies .... G. A. Henty
For the Temple .... G. A. Henty
A Knight of the White Cross... G. A. Henty
The Minute Boys of Lexington.. Edward Stratemeyer
The Minute Boys of Bunker Hill... Edward Stratemeyer
Hope and Have ....Oliver Optic
Taken by the Enemy, First in *The Blue and the Gray Series*............................... Oliver Optic
Within the Enemy's Lines, Second in *The Blue and the Gray Series*..................... Oliver Optic
On the Blockade, Third in *The Blue and the Gray Series*.. Oliver Optic
Stand by the Union, Fourth in *The Blue and the Gray Series* .... Oliver Optic
Fighting for the Right, Fifth in *The Blue and the Gray Series* .... Oliver Optic
A Victorious Union, Sixth and Final in *The Blue and the Gray Series* .... Oliver Optic
Mary of Plymouth ....James Otis

For more information visit us at: http://www.lostclassicsbooks.com